# Faster Than Wind

# Faster Than Wind

Steve Pitt

DUNDURN PRESS
TORONTO

Editor: Michael Carroll
Design: Courtney Horner
Printer: Webcom

**Library and Archives Canada Cataloguing in Publication**

Pitt, Steve, 1954-
Faster than wind : a novel / by Steve Pitt.

ISBN 978-1-55002-837-9

I. Title.

PS8631.I88F38 2008 jC813'.6 C2008-906214-0

1 2 3 4 5 13 12 11 10 09

Canada

We acknowledge the support of the **Canada Council for the Arts** and the **Ontario Arts Council** for our publishing program. We also acknowledge the financial support of the **Government of Canada** through the **Book Publishing Industry Development Program** and **The Association for the Export of Canadian Books**, and the **Government of Ontario** through the **Ontario Book Publishers Tax Credit program**, and the **Ontario Media Development Corporation**.

Care has been taken to trace the ownership of copyright material used in this book. The author and the publisher welcome any information enabling them to rectify any references or credits in subsequent editions.

*J. Kirk Howard, President*

Printed and bound in Canada.

www.dundurn.com

Dundurn Press
3 Church Street, Suite 500
Toronto, Ontario, Canada
M5E 1M2

Gazelle Book Services Limited
White Cross Mills
High Town, Lancaster, England
LA1 4XS

Dundurn Press
2250 Military Road
Tonawanda, NY
U.S.A. 14150

*To Jean and Bertie,*

*may there always be a warm sun over your heads*
*and a fair wind on your beam wherever you are*

# Acknowledgements

For details about iceboat construction and racing, I am deeply indebted to John Sperr of the Hudson River Ice Yacht Club; John Summers, chief curator of the Antique Boat Museum, Clayton, New York; Erich Schloemer, president of Midwest Rowing Ltd.; Deb Whitehorse, Four Lakes Ice Yacht Club in Wisconsin; and Richard Gerrard, registrar of Collections and Conservation Centre, Museum Services, City of Toronto. For sailing jargon, I thank my colleagues at the Saint James Town Sailing Club and apologize in advance for all the mistakes I likely made. For details about the CCM Russell automobile, I thank the Reverend Doug Wright of the United Church of Canada.

# 1

# Donnybrook at the Market

## December 24, 1906

“Paper!”

“Porcupines!”

“Paper!”

“Rabbits! Quail and porcupines!”

“Paper!”

“Grouse, wild geese, ducks, swans, quail, moose, venison, and … porcupines!”

I lowered my newspaper and looked behind me. “Has anyone ever actually bought a Christmas porcupine?” I asked Mr. Crane.

His long nose immediately swivelled and pointed directly at me like a spear. “I'm not out here hollering for my health!” he said, nearly breaking my eardrums.

Mr. Crane must have been doing something right for his health. He had been hawking wild game from the same stall in Toronto's St. Lawrence Market for sixty years. Barely five feet tall, he always stood ramrod straight, chest puffed out like the stuffed wild turkey perched on the roof of his stall. When he talked even to people two feet away, his voice almost knocked their hats off. His gruffness scared most of the other newspaper boys, but

Mr. Crane and I got along fine. I never interfered with his customers, and at the end of the day I handed him all my unsold newspapers to wrap his meats in. Some days, in return, he gave me a small piece of meat to take home to my mother. On other days he offered good advice. Today was an advice day.

"Run, Bertie!" his voice boomed like a starting pistol.

My feet were moving even before I saw the freckle-faced tide closing in on me from three directions. It was the Kellys, a gang of East Side toughs who wanted to hurt me very much.

There were seven daily newspapers in Toronto. Each had their own army of newsboys. If you knew how to hustle and had a good location, there was money to be made. Unfortunately, if you knew how to hurt and intimidate newspaper boys, there was even more money to grab. The Kellys did the latter. If any kid tried to sell newspapers on the East Side of the city, the Kelly Gang surrounded him and demanded half his money. If he refused, they beat him up and took all his money. Although I was small for a fifteen-year-old, I figured I could beat almost any Kelly in a one-on-one fight except their leader Sean, alias "Himself," who was huge for sixteen. But the Kellys never fought one-on-one. And as Sean always bragged with a smile, "You fight one Kelly, you're fighting all the Kellys."

Today it looked as if I was going to fight all of them. For the past three weeks I hadn't been paying my "rent." It wasn't just a silly principle thing. I really needed the money.

I turned right and saw five Kellys surging toward me with their fists clenched. I turned left and spotted five more. Straight in front were at least ten with Himself leading the attack.

With Mr. Crane's stall to my back, I was completely trapped. There was nothing to do but stand still and wait for the pounding to start. But then that "funny thing" happened again.

My brain liked to think it was the boss, but whenever my body got in trouble my hands and feet took over without asking. This had happened several times in my life already. For example, when I was six years old, a huge, angry dog charged me after it escaped from a dog catcher's wagon. My mind completely froze, but my hands, without my brain having the simplest clue what they were up to, calmly raised the umbrella I was carrying for my mother and aimed it point first at the stampeding animal like a rifle. Just as the mad mutt was about to sink its teeth into me, my right thumb released the spring catch that held the umbrella shut. The contraption flew open with a loud snap, and the dog ran yelping down the street with its tail between its legs. The dog catcher managed to huff out "Quick thinking, son!" as he chased the canine. *Smart thinking*? My brain had nothing to do with it. It was all in the hands.

But today I was facing something much worse than a mad dog. It was Sean Kelly. With my brain "watching" in disbelief, my hands suddenly dropped my newspapers and reached behind me. I felt something soft and furry. When I glanced down, I had a dead porcupine in each hand. I was holding each one by a front leg so that their long, bushy tails nearly touched the ground by my feet. I had no idea what I was going to do with them until the first Kelly, Hammy, made his move. He was a huge, round lump of a kid who got his nickname because even in winter his face was always red and shiny like a freshly boiled ham.

"Got 'em, Sean!" Hammy roared in triumph as he lunged for me.

My left hand snapped up, and we both stood there amazed as two dozen black and white needles suddenly appeared in Hammy's right hand and forearm. *"Aww-waww-waaaw!"* he keened in pain and horror.

Hughie Kelly, Sean's brother, closed in on my right side. In an earlier era Hughie's ancestors must have been hunted for their pelts, because he was the hairiest kid I had ever seen. Like his kin, Hughie was also dumber than a donkey cart full of doorknobs. He took one look at what I was gripping, stuck out his hand, and bellowed, "Gimme those!"

Two seconds later there were two Kellys screaming, *"Aww-waww-waaaw!"* The other gang members kept a wary distance, but I was still trapped.

The Kellys were well known in the market. All around me I could hear vendor stalls closing down. Doors slammed. Wooden screens rattled to the floor. Mr. Crane and the other vendors were shouting for the police, but it was unlikely the bulls would get here in time.

Judging by the relaxed smile on his face, Sean shared my opinion. "We're gonna kill you, McCross. You should have paid your rent when you had your chance."

Something tried to sneak up quietly on my right. Without taking my eyes off Sean, I flicked my right porcupine. A third voice joined the *"Aww-waww-*

*waaaw!"* chorus. One more and we'd have a barbershop quartet. Something moved to the left, and again I snapped a porcupine, but this time I missed. Even a Kelly could learn a new trick eventually.

At that point Sean's massive freckled head split in a grin. "Wrap your coats around your arms!" he ordered. After half a minute or so, most of the Kellys figured out what he meant. By wrapping their heavy leather and wool winter coats around their arms, they could fend off my porcupines, which were beginning to look pretty bald, anyway.

One by one they followed Sean's example. I watched them, feeling like one of those idiot Spartans my father had told me about — the three hundred who'd been tremendously outnumbered but who'd bravely held fast while they were annihilated by the archers of their enemies, the Persians. My father was always reading history books to me about brave people who stood their ground until they died and became famous. I preferred cheap westerns where the smart guys ran away and hid until the cavalry arrived and rescued them in the nick of time.

I didn't hear any bugles, but without warning both of my boots were sliding straight backward.

"Watch your head, Bertie!" Mr. Crane cried as he dragged me by the seat of my trousers under the bottom half of his stall door. *Ka-clunk!* went the door as he kicked it shut in the faces of two Kellys trying to follow.

"Over the screens!" Sean commanded, and immediately there was a thundering din as a dozen Kelly hobnailed boots began fighting their awkward way up over the stall walls.

At the back Mr. Crane's stall was connected to a small passageway that led to the aisle behind us. "Go out that way and run like heck!" he whispered to me. "And give me those!" He snatched back his porcupines.

I emerged out the back door just as the first Kellys came around the corner to the same aisle. Tipping over a delivery cart full of cheese wheels in their direction, I scrambled north.

My escape plan was to run down the main aisle of the market and out through the north doors to lose myself in the crowds of holiday shoppers on Front Street. It was a good scheme except for one thing. The merchants in the centre aisle were mostly bakers and confectioners. At this time of day their aisle was jammed with shoppers picking up last-minute Christmas orders.

I sidestepped a string of top-hatted carollers slow-marching through the market and singing "Deck the Halls." It was the carollers who got decked as a flying wedge of Kellys crashed through their centre, trying to catch up to me. As carollers scattered like bowling pins, I weaved my way toward the north doors.

Sean must have guessed my plan, because he sent some of his boys dashing up the less-crowded aisles on either side to head me off before I could reach my destination, now only twenty yards away. Fortunately, a tin-eared Salvation Army cornet player was doing a fine job of driving shoppers away from his kettle near the doors. In the clear, finally, I actually thought I was going to make it. Then two women pushing massive baby buggies locked bumpers and began insisting that the other go first through the doors.

*Blasted Canadians and their good manners!* I thought. My exit was blocked and I was about to be killed because somebody wanted to be polite.

There was no way out — only up!

The area near the north doors was nicknamed Little Berlin because it was dominated by stalls of German sausage makers. This year, to celebrate Christmas in the German tradition, they had all chipped in and erected a huge spruce in the middle of the aisle. It was covered in flags, streamers, waxed fruit, whirligigs, and other hideous gewgaws. When I told my father about it, he said it was a "Christmas tree," a tradition we had picked up from the British, who had gotten it from the Germans.

The tradition seemed like a really dumb idea to me. Who in his right mind wanted a dirty dead tree dragged inside his home just to hang fruit and tinsel on it until all the needles fell off and then have to haul it back out again? Some people even wired candles on them, lit them up, and then stood around with buckets of water ready to throw in case the tree caught fire. Rich people now put them up in their homes every Christmas, but I doubted the trees would ever catch on with sensible folk.

Anyway, with the Kellys closing in like a pack of freckled foxes, I did my best imitation of a Christmas squirrel. The bottom of the tree was anchored in a big wooden tub full of sand. For extra safety a piano wire was wrapped around the tree and connected to the ceiling near the top. I heard the wire go *twang!* like a banjo as soon as I started clawing my way up through the bottom branches.

Immediately below me I heard a whole lot of German cussing. At least I think it was cussing. It was hard to tell. Most German butchers sounded as if they were cussing even when they were just saying *"Guten morgen!"* to one another.

A dozen burly butchers fought to keep the Kellys from climbing up their tree after me. I heard Irish cussing mixed with the German. Fortunately, there were plenty of butchers to keep the Kellys under control. Just two of the smallest weaselly ones slipped through and scrabbled up the tree before they could be yanked down again. With three of us aboard, the tree shook violently and the wire at the top twanged higher and higher each time someone moved up a branch. Glass balls and whirligigs fell like bombs from the branches. Far below, breaking glass tinkled, and there was more German cussing. I peeked from the branches and a big greasy sausage just missed my head.

When I got near the top of the tree, a set of claws closed tightly around my right ankle. I looked down and saw a terrified freckled face peering up at me under the standard-issue Kelly mop of red hair. Using all my strength, I raised my right leg as high as I could. The Kelly grabbed my foot with one hand and started tugging. I didn't move. Getting nowhere with one hand, the Kelly let go of the tree to pull on my leg with both hands. As I said, Kellys were as dumb as doorknobs. As he tugged mightily, I let my leg slacken, and he began dropping backward. The Kelly then panicked and tried frantically to grasp the nearest tree branch but missed.

"Happy Christmas!" I shouted as he bounced down through the branches. *Thunk, ka-thunk, ka-thunk, ka-thunk,* he went, causing a glass-ornament blizzard. *Crash, tinkle, crunch, cuss, crash, tinkle, crunch, cuss, crash, tinkle, crunch, cuss.* The next Kelly was also right below me, but all on his own he didn't appear very brave. "Back off unless you want to join your brother on the floor," I warned.

"He's me cuzin," the Kelly said as if that made a difference.

Sean's voice growled up from below, "Get him, Pat, or I'll break your head for certain."

Facing a choice like that, Pat continued to climb. I still didn't want to fight, so I kept moving up until I ran out of tree. Pat and I were now at least forty feet from the market floor. Despite the dire situation, I still noticed that the view was quite breathtaking.

The whole market spread out below me like a miniature city festooned in all its Christmas glory. Gold-and-red-ribboned holly wreaths and mistletoe garlands hung everywhere. Underneath, hundreds of people stood still and gazed up at Pat and me with mixed expressions. Most pointed and laughed. Mr. Crane looked up with concern. Sean was down there, too, pacing like a terrier waiting for a rat to come out of its hole. A small army of German butchers surrounded the tree. Nearly all of them had at least one Kelly in a headlock or by the scruff of the neck. One stunningly pretty golden-haired girl my own age stood beside a suit of armour at a chocolate truffle stall. The beautiful girl was actually smiling at me. I was on the verge of tipping my hat to her when I heard an ominous noise three feet above my head.

*Biiiwoinnnnng!*

The wire holding the tree was starting to unravel. A couple of loose strands had popped out on the outside.

As the wire strained under our weight, the strands gently whirled like the legs of a ballet dancer. Pat began climbing the tree again, and the ballet turned into a jig as more "legs" appeared until the wire bounced and whirled like a dance-crazed octopus.

"Hey, stupid, stop it!" I yelled at Pat. "The wire's breaking."

"You get him, Pat, or else!" Sean growled from far below.

Reluctantly, Pat raised himself one more branch.

*Boinnnnnnnnnnng-whaaack!* went the wire as it finally snapped.

I clamped my legs and arms as tightly as I could around the treetop. With its roots firmly buried in the sand container below, and all our weight at the top, the tree flexed sideways like a gigantic fishing rod. We plunged toward Frau Dunkle's Famous Tripe, Tails, und Trotters stand. Our descent stopped abruptly as the tree reached the limit of its flex. Too dumb to hang on properly, Pat tumbled forward and landed face first in a bathtub-size vat of pickled pig parts. With him gone the tree snapped itself upright again, and I whipped backward in the other direction. The force of the reaction nearly hurled me off, and I thought I was going to plunge through the tent roof of Mrs. Dee's Fish and Chips, but the sight of a massive cauldron of bubbling hot grease helped my hands and legs to find the strength to hang on. Like a piano teacher's metronome, the tree rocked me back and forth several times between the gut tubs and hot grease, but gradually momentum was lost and I came to a halt.

Heaving a long sigh of relief, my whole body trembling from nerves and the physical strain, I was aware enough to be amazed that the golden-haired girl was still standing there, her mouth gaping. I no longer had a hat to tip, so I gave her a wink and raised my hand to salute. As soon as my hand reached my head, there was a loud snap and the tree trunk broke, pitching me off.

My fall wasn't as painful as I thought it would be. Each branch broke or gave way enough to slow me down, and my heavy winter clothes absorbed most of the shock. Of course, when I hit the floor it would be a different story. The floor was solid hardwood. I closed my eyes, clenched my teeth, and prepared for a spine-cracking impact.

*Whummmph!* I smacked the floor, but something else broke my fall. Two teenagers had locked arms and caught me in their arms. They deliberately collapsed under my weight, and we slumped to the floor in a tangle.

"Nice catch, Tommy," the shorter one said.

"Good idea, Ed," the other answered. Then they began laughing because we were covered head to foot with sawdust from the butcher stalls.

I didn't laugh. More Kellys were coming straight at me, with Sean leading the pack, his fist raised.

"Where you goin', Pumpkin Head?" the teen called Tommy said, stepping between Sean and me, still smiling as if he had just heard the best joke of the year.

Sean came to a dead stop. No one had ever dared call him Pumpkin Head to his face. "Out of my way. I'm going to kill that little pug."

"I don't think so," Tommy said. "We just saved him, and that would make Ed and me look like chumps, seeing how we just took a sawdust bath for our trouble. Right, Ed?"

"*Ppppah!* I even got some in my mouth," Ed agreed, spitting and making a big show of whacking the sawdust off my coat with his tattered cap.

"This isn't your business," Sean snarled, trying to look menacing.

"I'm making it my business, Carrot Top," Tommy said without the least bit of menace in his voice, but even Sean had enough sense to be wary.

Ed and Tommy were familiar sights around the market. Tommy lived on one of the islands in Toronto's harbour and made his living from fishing and sailing with his father. Although he was still only sixteen, he already had a prizefighter's build from a lifetime of rowing and hauling sails seven days a week.

Milwaukee Ed, as he was known, was pretty formidable himself. No one knew his exact age because he was an orphan. In 1891 Grand Trunk Railway workers found him as a tiny baby in a boxcar nestled in a crate marked MILWAUKEE EDGED TOOL MANUFACTORY, with just a handwritten note that said "Please take care of him." Because there was no name in the note, the dock-wallopers dubbed him Milwaukee Ed after the crate they discovered him in.

Ed grew up sleeping on a shelf in a railway tool shed and unloaded crates in return for leftovers from workmen's lunch pails. When he was twelve or so, Ed found a steady job on the market docks, which was where he met Tommy. The two became fast friends, and when they weren't working, they were always seen together.

Sean made one more move to go around Tommy, who said, "Back off — hey, Ed, I need another orange vegetable."

Ed shrugged. "Beats me."

"How about yam?" I offered.

"Yam?" Ed, Tommy, and Sean echoed, staring at me in puzzlement.

"You know, a sweet potato."

Tommy flashed me an impressed smile, then looked Sean in the eye. "Oh, sure, perfect. Back off there ... Sweet ... Potato."

The crowd around us erupted in laughter.

Sean's skull nearly exploded as he struggled to contain his rage. As a gang leader, he had a reputation to maintain, but he hadn't become the East Side's top hooligan by picking fights he couldn't win. Tommy knew that, too. He even turned his back on Sean to pick some imaginary sawdust off my coat. "Sweet potato. I'll be —" he started to say to me.

Then someone shouted, "The bulls are coming!" And suddenly the market was filled with the thunder of heavy boots.

"We'll get you, McCross," Sean snarled at me as he melted into the crowd. "Count on it!"

2

# Iceboat Initiation

## December 24, 1906

For fifteen minutes the stall merchants complained long and bitterly to the police about the constant trouble newspaper boys caused. To the cops it was just one more paragraph in a long story. Nearly every day there was a complaint somewhere about newsies. We were just poor kids trying to make a living, but to established merchants we were one step lower than skunks raiding the garbage.

"Who's going to pay for this mess?" the market manager demanded, pointing at the hundreds of broken Christmas ornaments.

"They knocked over my cheese wheels!"

"My tripe and trotters are ruined!" Mrs. Dunkle shrieked.

"I've got six feet of spruce stuck in my deep fryer!" Mrs. Dee cried.

I wasn't going anywhere. One of the cops had me by the neck. At the very least I suspected I was going to spend Christmas Eve in jail. Several of the Kellys who hadn't escaped the butchers would likely be joining me. None of us would have a silent, holy night.

"This lad here didn't do anything!" Mr. Crane insisted.

A butcher named Graffman scowled. "Him? He started the whole thing!"

"He was running away from those Kelly thugs!" Mrs. Weekes, a flower stall vendor, added. "They're always hurting people."

"Bertie's a good lad," Mr. Crane said, pointing at me.

"He's telling the truth, Jack," Tommy said.

Jack seemed to give Tommy's opinion considerable weight. He looked down at me like a bored cat clutching a rodent with his paw, trying to decide whether to let me go or bite my head off. "I hate newspaper kids," he finally muttered.

"*Royal George* looks good for Boxing Day, Jack," Tommy said quietly.

"What are the odds?" the cop asked.

"Three to one on Phelan's *IT*."

"So then why *Royal George*?"

"Phelan wins when the wind's up. *Royal George* wins when the wind's down."

"You think it'll be down?"

"Wind's blowing strong from the west tonight," Tommy said. "That usually means a lull for a day or two afterward. Three to one *Royal George*."

Jack released a long, beery sigh. "What's your name, boy?"

"Bertie McCross, sir."

"McCross?"

"Yes, sir."

"Where do you go to school?"

"Parkdale Public, sir."

Jack and the other policeman exchanged glances. The powerful hand gripping me let go of my collar, and my heels touched the floor for the first time in five minutes.

"Okay, McCross," Jack said. "This is your first, last, and only warning. Stay out of my beat. Go peddle your papers in Parkdale."

"Yes, sir."

"And if I ever see you again, you'll be getting a taste of this," Jack said, smacking a lead-weighted nightstick hard against his hand.

"Yes, sir."

"But the rest of you pikeys are going to lockup," Jack growled. "If you're lucky, you'll get out by St. Valentine's Day."

The Kellys were frog-marched out between the cops and a posse of butchers. I scanned the crowd for Sean, but he was long gone. I noticed the blond girl again giving me one final look. Then what I had thought was a suit of armour suddenly moved. The metal suit turned out to be a woman in a silver dress. Her starched silk dress looked so much like sheets of metal that I fully expected to hear it squeak and clank as she hustled the beautiful blond girl away. My eyes followed them to the door, and when the young lady glanced back and smiled one last time, I felt blood rush to my face.

"You'd better go home, Bertie!" Mr. Crane suggested, suddenly smiling. He had seen me gazing at the young girl. His voice brought me back to reality.

As I thanked Mr. Crane and the flower lady for standing up for me, I saw Tommy and Ed heading out the south doors. I ran after them. "Hey!" I cried.

"Hey, yourself," Ed answered.

"Thanks a lot. You saved me — twice."

"You made the day ... different," Tommy said.

"I always seem to do that for people whether I want to or not."

Tommy laughed. "Yeah, you climb pretty good there, kid."

"Hey, Tommy, we could use him," Ed said.

"What?"

"For the race crew. Did you see the way he hanged on?"

"Hung on," I said. I had my father's unfortunate habit of correcting people's bad English.

Tommy and Ed looked at me funny and then broke out laughing. "Well, he can sure climb, but he'd probably still be scared silly," Tommy said.

"He just took on the whole Kelly clan and is still standing," Ed said.

"You're right. He might have some guts."

I had no idea what they were talking about, but I wasn't anxious to leave, with Sean and what was left of his gang likely still out there.

"What's your name, anyway?" Tommy asked.

"Bertie."

"Bert, you ever been on an iceboat?"

"No," I told Tommy, "but before tonight I'd never climbed a Christmas tree, either."

Tommy laughed. "He's crazy."

Ed grinned. "We need crazy."

"You're right." Tommy put a hand on my shoulder.

"C'mon, Bertie, we've got something to show you."

With Ed and Tommy as my escorts, we walked out the south door. The St. Lawrence Market used to sit right on the waterfront. Now much of the shoreline had been extended south with landfill, but a water canal had been left so that small boats from Lake Ontario could still sail up almost to the foot of the market to deliver their goods. At this time of year all the water between the Toronto shoreline and the islands was frozen solid. The silhouettes of several cabbage heads bobbed in the shadows as we walked south, crossed some railway tracks, slid down a steep bank, and strode out onto the frozen canal.

Parked in the ice channel was a large wooden contraption that looked as if a sailboat had collided with a horse sleigh. It was an iceboat. All my life I had seen them dashing across Toronto's harbour at incredible speeds. My father had told me that with the right wind they were the fastest vehicles on earth. They certainly seemed to crash more than any other vehicles on earth. In the wintertime the newspapers were full of stories about races and crashes. Many people were injured every year. Sometimes someone even died.

"This is the *Marinion*," Tommy said. "Want to take a ride?"

I was scared spitless, but with a shoreline full of Kellys still waiting for me, I said, "Love to."

"Climb aboard," Tommy urged.

"Where?" I asked.

"Up here," Ed said, indicating a tiny triangular-shaped platform at the rear end of the boat.

"Can all three of us fit up there?"

"Are you kidding?" Ed said. "On a race day there's five or more onboard."

"You guys race?" I asked as I climbed into the box.

"Yep," Tommy said. "Hang on!"

I felt the back end of the boat lift as Tommy and Ed picked up the vessel and flipped the rear runner so that a metal skate faced down onto the ice. Then they climbed aboard and began yanking ropes and spinning pulleys. A sail rose suddenly like a shark fin, and when the wind caught it, the boat started to move. We sailed out of the water channel and into the main harbour.

The *Marinion* increased speed rapidly until we were going as fast as a galloping horse. In the moonlight I thought I could see some shadowy Kellys riding double and triple on bicycles racing along the eastern shore in a vain attempt to keep up with us, but they were soon left behind.

Wind whistled in the rigging overhead, and the blades on the ice made a dull, roaring sound as the boat glided along. We were sailing southeast toward the Toronto Islands. The islands were actually a collection of sandbars that protected Toronto's harbour from the big waves of Lake Ontario. Some people, like Tommy, lived on the islands year-long, but mostly they were deserted in the winter. It was because of the islands that Toronto's harbour froze over, forming a perfect iceboat racetrack.

Sometimes the ride on the boat was so smooth I thought we had come to a halt except that objects on the ice suddenly whizzed past as if they had been fired out of a cannon. Other times we'd hit some rough ice and I'd feel my teeth rattle as the boat shuddered violently and I had to cling tightly to the platform to keep myself from being thrown off.

*Bang!*

Without warning the boat leaped off the ice and landed hard a dozen yards later.

"What the heck was that?" I asked.

Tommy shrugged. "Pressure crack. The wind and the currents cause the ice to shift. They cause a ridge to form and they're hard to see at night. No worry unless the winds open the ice and we fall through a hole."

"Can you swim?" Ed asked me.

"Yes."

"Too bad," Ed said. "That water's so cold that if we fell in we'd be dead in less than a minute, anyway." Both he and Tommy laughed.

Yes, I thought, crazy was definitely a good thing to be on this contraption.

The easternmost island, Ward's, suddenly loomed very close. That meant we had crossed half a mile of ice in a matter of seconds. Tommy turned the tiller bar hard, and the boat swung with a spray of ice and creaking wood. The thick wooden beam that ran along the bottom of the sail swung straight at us like a huge baseball bat. It stopped just inches from my face. Tommy and Ed ducked without even appearing to think about it and began pulling ropes and readjusting the sail. In a few more seconds we were heading back toward the city.

"Switch sides, Bertie," Ed said. "You're slowing us down."

Carefully, I ducked under the beam and sat on the opposite side of the boat.

"Where do you live?" Tommy asked.

"Over by the old fort. But the wind's going the wrong way. We'll never get there."

"Not a problem," Tommy said as he turned the craft west. Now the wind was almost against us.

The boat appeared to be moving even faster. We hit a few more pressure ridges, only this time we seemed to barely feel them. We just sailed over the gaps. The wind was hitting our sail from the left, making the left forward runner occasionally lift off the ice.

"Hang on and c'mon up," Ed said as he stood and started moving forward on the boat.

"What?" I asked.

"C'mon. Let's see what the old girl will do tonight."

Following Ed's lead, I stood. Just two feet below, the ice continued to roll past faster than a horse could run. Ed was already halfway up the boat. Looking from above, an iceboat was constructed like a cross. At the bottom of the cross was the small platform where Tommy, Ed, and I had been sitting. Where the platform ended, all there was to stand on was a wooden beam about ten inches wide. It led to the front where an even thinner crossbeam went out about ten feet on either side. That was where the mast also rose. The sail billowed out to the right. Clinging to a skinny rope, I inched forward one baby step at a time until I reached the crossbeam. Ed was already out on the left crossbeam, holding on to another skinny rope that ran from the boat's left blade to the top of the mast. I felt as if I were the bravest guy in the world just getting as far forward as the mast.

*Bang!* We hit another pressure crack. My head bumped hard against the mast. I looked over my shoulder, expecting to see an empty space where Ed had been standing, but he was still there, leaning back with his legs flexed.

"C'mon, Bertie!" Ed called "Best ride in the country!"

I glanced down.

"Don't look down," Ed immediately said.

"Just grab the rope and step out!" Tommy called from behind.

My legs felt like jelly. As skinny as that main beam was, it seemed like a boardwalk compared to the crossbeam. But if Ed could do it, so could I. With my left hand I reached up and grabbed the rope that ran from the mast to the runner. With my left foot I groped about until I felt the side beam underneath me. Gingerly, I shifted my weight from my right leg to my left, then extended my right hand and grabbed the rope.

"That's the way!" Ed said. "You're a natural!" He nudged me in the ribs with his elbow "What a view, eh?"

"Yeah!" I said. From where Ed was standing he couldn't see that both my eyes were closed.

"Nothing to it," Ed murmured.

Until I stepped out, the left crossbeam had been bucking like an irritable bronco. Now the *Marinion* was running smoothly along the ice, and I could finally force myself to open my eyes. I saw that we were now about fifty yards from shore, running neck and neck with a westbound express train. I could see people in the passenger cars reading newspapers and talking while we overtook them and pulled ahead.

"Hang on!" Tommy yelled as the wind suddenly increased and the left runner hiked up again.

As the blade left the ice, Ed and I leaned back to keep the craft from tipping. It was the most terrifying experience of my life — and I never felt so happy. Memories of the Kellys, the cops, the whole rotten last year of my life seemed to peel away one layer at a time.

The light at the end of Queen's Wharf seemed to race right at us. Tommy adjusted the sail, and the boat instantly slowed down. Twenty yards from shore he let the sail drop altogether, and we coasted gently to a stop.

"My legs feel wobbly," I said as I stepped down onto the ice.

"Does that mean you don't want to race then?" Ed asked.

"Heck, no!" I said. "I mean, yes! I want to race."

"Then come to the foot of York Street on Boxing Day," Tommy said. "We'll be racing with my father, but he's almost finished his new boat, the *King Edward*. As soon as he's done, the *Marinion* will be mine and I'll need my own crew."

"I'll see you on Boxing Day," I promised.

"We'll be looking for you," Tommy said as he and Ed picked up the tail of the *Marinion* and turned the boat to face the lake again. They climbed aboard and dropped the sail. "Race starts at noon!" Tommy shouted as they faded into the darkness. "Come early and we'll give you a sailing lesson."

The ground felt suddenly strange under my feet as I walked up the wharf toward Bathurst Street. I turned left at Niagara Street and continued northwest along the silent roads. My neighbourhood was a jumble of failing businesses and dilapidated little houses full of overworked people. From a stockyard nearby I heard the sad lowing of doomed cattle. My home was a tiny red-and-yellow-brick cottage on Defoe Street that looked as if at one time it had been a farmhouse all on its own in the country, but now it was sandwiched between a Chinese laundry and a stable belonging to a knacker named Hacker who collected and disposed of dead livestock.

Because it was Christmas Eve, both the laundry and dead animal smells were absent for once as I trudged around the last corner. A light snow had fallen. No lights were visible from inside the house as I swept our three sagging wooden steps with a nearly bald broom. Then I took a minute to enjoy the rare fresh air and study the few stars that could penetrate the tangle of naked tree branches overhead. It was hard to believe that this was the same sky I once looked up at from the grand porch of our "good" house over in Parkdale.

After a last deep breath, I opened the front door and was nearly knocked over by the smell of something burning. Either the horsehair couch in the parlour was on fire or my mom was cooking again. The former was definitely preferable. Father sometimes let his pipe ashes fall onto the furniture, and my mom was probably the worst cook in Toronto, if not Canada. I had to step carefully. The hallway was dark and so crammed with oversize furniture that it was like crawling through a cavern without a torch. Groping with my hands, I finally found my way into the parlour.

"Evening, Bertie," said a muffled voice from the corner. I could smell pipe tobacco. No other fire was visible, so I figured Mom must be destroying dinner.

If a visitor ever had to describe our front parlour, he would be hard-pressed to say whether the room was painted or papered, since every inch of wall space was covered by makeshift shelves straining under the weight of fine leather books. Nor could that same person likely tell what time of day he was visiting because the bay window looking out into the front yard was bricked up floor to ceiling with more books. Still more books rose like twisting stalagmites from the floor. Over the only piece of visible furniture in the room, Father's wing chair, several huge stacks of books had collapsed together to form an arch. Father was sitting under the arch with a book open on his lap and a handkerchief in his right hand. He was already in uniform, his shoes perfectly polished, but his freshly shaved cheeks were wet with tears. Christmas Eve or not, he had to leave for work in two hours.

"How you feeling, Father?"

"Fine, son, fine," he said, wiping his cheeks with the handkerchief. He smiled weakly, and after a few awkward seconds, dabbed his cheek again.

I smiled back. "What are you reading?"

He held up a thick orange leather book. "*On Snowshoes to the Barren Grounds: Twenty-Eight Hundred Miles After Musk Ox and Wood Bison* by Lieutenant Caspar Whitney, Royal Navy."

"Is it good?"

"Can't tell yet. I'm only on page fifty-seven."

Father usually took at least a couple of hundred pages to decide whether he liked a book or not.

"Right now Lieutenant Caspar's describing how he's trying to prepare himself for Arctic camping by sleeping outside on a normal English winter night with only one blanket. He's been at it a week, and so far he's done more shivering than sleeping."

"He must want to go to the Arctic pretty badly," I said.

"It would sure be something exciting to do," Father said with a faraway expression. "The farthest north I've ever been is Calgary and that was by train. I'd sure love to go somewhere someday on snowshoes." He dabbed his eyes again.

Not very long ago my father had been the general manager of one of the biggest bicycle companies in Canada. He had travelled a lot and had made heaps of money. But he had also worried about things like the price of steel, the shortage of leather, and whether he should order more of something today or wait until next week in case the price per ton went up or down a few cents.

His decisions had been important because the lives of many people had depended on them. The bicycle business was quite competitive, and if someone like him made the wrong decision, people lost their jobs. If it rained a lot, people stopped buying bikes and workers were laid off. If the company made blue bikes and customers decided that year they wanted red, workers were laid off. Sometimes the company's board of directors would tell Father to close a profitable factory because they had bought another one where people were willing to work for less money. Father's real passion was designing things, and he hated the pressure of being responsible for making decisions that affected workers' lives.

One day he started to cry. No reason. In the middle of a conversation with his production manager about laying people off, the tears gushed and he couldn't stop them. He hid in his office and bawled for four hours. He came home by horse cab and cried throughout the night. He went back to work the next day, but the tears kept flowing. The board of directors became very concerned.

They told him, "Your services are no longer required." And suddenly my father no longer made bicycles. With my father not working we soon had to leave our big home on Dunn Avenue in Parkdale and move to this tiny house. Eventually, Father found a job as a night watchman in a ten-floor warehouse on Spadina Avenue where he worked six nights a week with no time off on holidays. He still cried, but no one could see him except us, so he figured that was okay. He also got to read at work.

When he worked at the bicycle factory, he never had time to read, though he still brought home a new book every week. At least with the new job he was able to read. My mom didn't really like the way the books took up most of the house, but she didn't say anything because when Father read he stopped crying.

At the warehouse Father just had to stay awake in case someone tried to break in. To prove he didn't sleep through his shift, he had to carry a clock apparatus on a long leather sling around his neck. On each floor of the warehouse there were two keys, each chained to the wall at opposite ends of the floor. Every hour my father had to walk through the entire building and punch each key into the clock. In the morning the warehouse owner looked at the clock to see what time each key had been punched. If there were any spaces on the time paper, my father would lose his job.

To stay awake all night, Father taught himself to read while he walked. He took the freight elevator to the top floor and punched the first key, then turned around and stepped toward the other side of the warehouse, reading as he strolled. When he bumped into the far side, he punched the other key and then went down a flight of stairs and began again. It worked most of the time, but occasionally he came home with a black eye or a bruised shin from bumping into things. Once he even fell down a fire escape. He returned home looking as if a horse had kicked him. "I got off lucky," he had told Mom and me, holding up the book he was reading. "Look, not a scratch."

"Father, I had an iceboat ride today," I said now as I peeled off my sweater.

"Iceboats? They were invented by the Dutch, you know."

*Only my father would know something like that,* I thought.

Before I could say anything else, Mom walked into the room. "Why does it smell like a forest in here?"

"Bertie had an iceboat ride today, Mildred."

"Then why is he covered in pine needles and sap?"

"It's a long story." I told them what happened except for the porcupines.

"Well, your days as a newspaper boy are over," my mom said as she scrubbed the pine tar off my face in the bathroom.

"We need the money, Ma," I reminded her.

"Do not call me Ma. I'm your mother. We need money, yes, but we don't need it if it's going get you killed. Climbing a Christmas tree. Riding an iceboat. Well, I never!"

"But —" I began, but a soapy washcloth got jammed in my mouth.

"No buts. You're not going back to that market. You'll either end up hurt by those Kelly mutts or arrested by the police. Don't worry. We'll get by and something else will turn up."

And something did turn up, but not a job. That night a small package wrapped in brown butcher's paper arrived with a note. It said: "Merry Christmas. Tastes like chicken. L. Crane, Butcher and Purveyor of Fine Wild Game."

"What on earth are they?" my mom asked when she opened the package. Inside were two freshly cleaned animal carcasses.

"Rabbits perhaps?" Father suggested.

"And it looks as if they've been tenderized already," my mom said. "What a dear man."

I nodded. If you ever needed to tenderize a porcupine, all you had to do was find the nearest Kelly.

Because Mom had destroyed dinner, I offered to cook the "rabbits." I had become a much better cook than my mom just by watching the food vendors at work at the market. I cut up the porcupines into small pieces, dredged them in flour, salt, and pepper and then braised them with onions, preserved tomatoes, and dried rosemary the way I had watched Mrs. Giancarlo, an Italian cook, prepare leftover game from Mr. Crane's stall.

I knew Mom was embarrassed that she couldn't cook, but it wasn't fair. Until my father had lost his job, my poor mother had never lifted a frying pan or sifted a cup of flour in her life. As the daughter of an Anglican minister, she had been trained by her mother and her finishing school to supervise servants. She knew exactly what went into beef bourguignon, but she couldn't peel a carrot without doing herself harm. Her once beautiful ivory hands were now red from harsh soap, stove burns, and festering knife cuts, but she never complained. Her family in England still had no idea what had happened to us. "No need to worry them," Mom always insisted. "Things will get better."

The porcupines were delicious except that they tasted more like pork than chicken. I guess that was why French Canadians named them pin-pigs. We had a quiet Christmas Eve dinner. Afterward, Father read to us about Lieutenant Caspar shivering in his blanket. Then it was time for him to go to work and for us to go to bed.

That night I dreamed I was sailing alone across Toronto's frozen bay on a huge iceboat that, instead of a mast, had a huge Christmas tree bending into the breeze. Porcupines and German sausages swung in the branches. And somewhere in the breeze a Christmas chorus of Kellys went *"Aww-waww-waaaw!"*

3

# Boxing Day

## December 26, 1906

It was a fine, bright winter day when I arrived at the foot of York Street where Tommy and Ed had said they parked their iceboat. The harbour ice was packed with people.

Every early December, as the temperature dropped below freezing, ice started forming on Toronto Bay. By late December, the ice was thick enough for fully loaded horse wagons to drive from shore to the Toronto Islands. Almost overnight the waterfront was transformed from a deserted wasteland into a bustling winter playground. Along the shoreline an official promenade was marked out that ran parallel to Front Street. Here warmly dressed pleasure walkers strolled arm in arm, tipping their hats to friends and acquaintances. Taxi drivers hitched up their horses to old-fashioned sleighs and offered rides to tourists. Even the occasional horseless carriage was spotted chugging along the promenade, horns honking in greeting. Food vendors quickly followed, setting up booths offering hot drinks, popcorn, sausage sandwiches, and roasted chestnuts.

A short way out young boys earned a fast nickel by shovelling snow to create curling rinks for older people or skating circles where young couples slowly skated in circles together or single young men showed off their skating skills for admiring girls to watch. Farther from shore small armies of other young men cleared off large squares of ice to play hockey games that lasted a whole day, with scores running into triple digits.

Amid all that hubbub, iceboats scudded back and forth like swordfish among small fry. When they weren't racing, many iceboat crews earned a quarter or two giving one-way rides to and from the Toronto Islands or tours around the harbour in their craft. The islands were about a half-mile from the foot of York Street, the place where the iceboats usually parked. If the wind was right, the iceboaters wagered with their customers that they could carry them to the islands in less than a minute or the ride was free. For the family-minded, iceboats offered slower full circles around the harbour for ten cents a passenger, five passengers minimum.

The ice south of York Street was crowded with boat masts and sailing crews all waiting for fares. The sailors sat around bonfires built on scraps of iron to keep warm. I didn't see the *Marinion* parked with the other boats, then I spied Tommy and Ed slowly zigzagging around the ice with four delighted, screaming children and two nervous parents onboard.

"Looking for a ride, son?" an elderly man asked hopefully.

"No thanks," I said. "I've got one already."

The man nodded and returned to chatting with his friends.

Eventually, the *Marinion* returned to the iceboat anchorage and gracefully coasted to a halt. Climbing out, the mother began counting out sixty cents in dimes, nickels, and pennies into Tommy's hand. Both adults seemed grateful to be standing on ice again, but there was a mutiny on the *Marinion* when the four children were informed that the ride was over. Their screams of protest drowned out the seagulls competing for sausage scraps from the nearby garbage cans.

"Sorry, kids, ride's over," Ed said, trying to help the father lift the children out of the cockpit. The two oldest were twins, set apart only by the fact that each had identical snot trails running down their chins from opposite nostrils. When lifted out of the *Marinion*, they wailed in unison and kicked snow at their father and Ed. As soon as the third child's feet touched the snow, he threw himself onto the ice and began spinning like a pinwheel as he threw a tantrum.

"Yipes!" Ed yelped.

The last child clamped both his arms and leg around Ed's right arm. "I wanna 'nother ride!" he shrieked.

"Watch out!" the father warned, trying to pick the pinwheel kid out of the snow. "That one's a biter."

"A biter?" Ed repeated, genuinely frightened. "*Ouch!* He *is* biting."

"Naw, he's just pinching, mister," one of the smirking twins said.

*"Ouch!"* Ed shouted. "I don't care. Hey, Bertie! Get this lobster off me! *Ouch!*"

The other twin laughed. "Now he's gonna bite."

The mother was still counting out sixty cents in nickels and pennies into Tommy's hand while I tried to pry Lobster Brat off Ed's arm. Just as I got both hands loose, he lunged with his teeth and snagged Ed's jacket just above the elbow. "Hey, that's new!" Ed protested.

*"Har-Arrrrrrrrrr,"* the kid snarled through clenched teeth. *"Woof! Woof! Woof!"*

"He's playing woof-woof now," one of the twins said.

"Woof-woof?" Ed questioned.

"Woof-Woof is our bulldog," the first twin said. "He bites mailmen."

*"Har-Arrrrrrrrrr,"* the kid growled.

"And milkmen," the other twin said. "He even bit a policeman once, and then he died."

"Who?" Ed rasped. "The policeman?"

"No, Woof-Woof!" the twins said together.

For a little guy the kid was really strong. It was all I could do to keep him from getting more than just a piece of Ed's coat.

"Eliot, let go of the nice man's arm and I promise we'll come back sometime for another ride!" the father said, struggling to stand the pinwheel child upright. But the kid kept flopping over and spinning his feet.

*"Woof! Woof!"*

*"Eliot!"* the father screamed.

*"Woof! Woof! Woof!"*

The woman finished counting the money. She glanced over at Eliot and snapped her purse shut. Suddenly, the whole bay seemed to go quiet.

"Eliot, let go of that man's arm right now," she said in a barely audible voice.

Eliot immediately let go of Ed's arm. I put him down in the snow, and he stood there, spitting brown bits of coat fluff out of his mouth.

"Say thank you to the nice men for the ride," the mother commanded.

"Thank you," the four boys and the father said in unison.

"We hope to see you again," the woman said sweetly as they walked away.

"Not if we see you first," Ed said under his breath as he tried to rub the teeth marks out of his coat.

"Wow!" I said. "You get many fares like that?"

Ed scowled. "No. Some are worse."

"Ready for your first sailing lesson?" Tommy asked me.

"Can't wait."

"Then your chariot awaits, m'lord," Ed said with a bow and a wave of his arm.

We turned the *Marinion* around. Following Ed's example, I stood behind the right runner while Tommy positioned himself at the back of the boat. On Tommy's command all three of us pushed the craft forward. Once we got the boat moving, Tommy jumped in and pulled on the rope that raised the sail.

"Okay, Bertie, here we go," Ed said, leaping in as the boat moved forward under its own power.

The sun was shining and the wind was strong, so we were able to put in two hours of sailing where I literally learned "the ropes" of iceboat racing. The first thing I found out was that ropes were called anything but ropes on an iceboat. The ropes that held up the mast from the sides were shrouds, the ones that braced the mast from the front and back were stays, the ones that ran into the rigging so that someone could climb to the top of the mast were ratlines, the one that raised the sail was a halyard, and the one that controlled the sail was a sheet.

Everything on a boat had a different name than I was used to. The front of the boat was the bow and the back was the stern. Left was port and right was starboard. When Tommy turned the boat, that was called tacking or gybing, depending on whether the wind was in front or behind us.

Both gybing and tacking involved ducking under the big swinging stick on the bottom of the sail as it lurched from one side of the boat to the other. It was appropriately named a boom because if you didn't duck quickly enough, it hit you in the head. *Boom!*

Besides moving our weight from one side of the boat to the other, part of the job for the crew was to look out for bad ice, open water, and deadheads, which were logs, boards, or any big pieces of garbage frozen into the ice that stuck up high enough to do damage. If the sailing was smooth, I climbed a few rungs on the ratlines because the view was better up there.

Not surprisingly, sometimes when the boat zigged, I zagged because I didn't grab a handhold fast enough. That sent me tumbling off the boat, though I didn't have far to fall. Usually, I just skidded across the ice, hoping I wouldn't hit anything until I came to a rest.

At noon there were three races staged with at least ten boats per contest. I stood on the shore and watched as Ed, Tommy, and Tommy's father, Hector, competed in the second and third races.

The racecourse was set up like a triangle, with the starting point and finish line at the foot of York Street.

There was a marker set in the ice at the Eastern Gap of Toronto harbour and another one at the Western Gap. A triangular course meant that the racers usually had one leg with the wind solidly behind them, a second leg where the wind was at their side, and a third leg where they had to sail into the wind. Sailing into the wind demanded the greatest skills because the boats had to tack back and forth. That was difficult enough when an iceboat was alone on the ice, but it was really challenging when there were up to a dozen boats zigzagging in a tight clump. Collisions were frequent, and sometimes boats were so badly damaged that they had to be dragged back to the finish line by a team of horses.

The *Royal George* won the first race, just as Tommy had predicted. In the second race the *Marinion* placed third, but in the last heat of the day it won and the crew collected a five-dollar prize from a purse that had been created by all the entrants contributing a dollar each.

After the races, we went out for a few more laps around the bay so I could practise standing on the runner beam. I was getting better; I only fell off once. Before we knew it we could hear the clock bells in the New City Hall ringing 4:30 p.m. Darkness came early to Toronto in December. With the sun setting in the west, we sailed back to the York Street anchorage, which was again crowded with boats. During the weekdays, less than ten boats were parked here. Most belonged to professional ice taxi drivers who made their living transporting people to and from the different islands. On the weekends as many as fifty boats crowded the ice. The majority of the weekend skippers were amateurs in clunky homemade boats, but there were also rich people with fancy custom-made craft.

When the iceboat sailors weren't out on the ice, they sat on wooden buckets and packing crates around open campfires — millionaires rubbing shoulders with common working men. They exchanged sailing stories, relived past races, and told jokes, mostly about sailing and races. Blackened iron kettles full of melted snow continuously hissed over the fire for tea, and from a fifty-pound burlap bag sailors threw unpeeled potatoes onto the coals, which they turned with long sticks until the coals were completely black. Each boat had a small store of tea bags and tin cups, and anyone could help themselves to the kettle water or a hot potato.

Like most old hands, Tommy and Ed could pick a potato right out of the fire and hold it in their bare fingers. The first time I tried it I burned myself.

*"Ouch! Ouch! Ouch!"* I gasped, letting the spud land with a hiss on the snow. This earned me a loud burst of laughter from the rest of the men.

"Here, laddie," a gruff old man said, handing me a long spruce stick he had been whittling for kindling. I stuck it in the spud and lifted it out of the snow. Steam poured off the potato, but it quickly cooled until I thought it was safe to take a bite.

"Hot! Hot!" I cried, burning my mouth. But after a full day of sailing, the spud tasted wonderful — even the burnt parts.

"Don't forget the pepper and salt," Ed said, producing two tiny shakers from his coat pocket.

I found an empty nail barrel and sat on it crosswise.

"How did you boys do for fares today?" a fuzzy-jawed young captain asked Tommy.

"Two one-way island runs and one round-the-harbour tour," Tommy replied.

"We had a good one," another skipper said. "Five young lasses from the nursing school. Lots of ankle."

A third captain jabbed his colleague's ribs hard. "Tender lugs about, Simon. Watch your language."

I blushed not from the comment but from the fact that some of these men obviously thought of me as a child.

"So who's your new man there, Captain McDonell?" a silver-haired man in his forties asked Tommy.

"Fred, this is Bertie McCross," Tommy said. "Bertie, this is Fred Phelan."

Both Fred and I half stood so we could shake hands. As someone at another campfire started playing an accordion, Ed filled me in on who was sitting around our circle tonight.

Fred Phelan was the undisputed iceboat king in Toronto Harbour. He had a custom-made racing boat simply known as *IT*. Because he was a high-ranking member of the Queen City Yacht Club, they called him the Vice Commodore. Next to Phelan was Tommy's father, Hector McDonell. Fred and Hector were considered the best iceboat racers in the city. While Fred had a reputation for winning through iron nerve, Hector was known for his tactical skill. He never made a false move on the ice and often prevailed over faster, more daring skippers who came to grief after taking one chance too many. It was Hector's reputation for stability that earned him the honour of introducing Canada's governor general, Earl Grey, to iceboat racing.

Governor General Grey was known for his love of sports, especially rugby, which was a pretty rough game, but for his first iceboat race the Canadian government selected Hector McDonell's craft because of the man's record for safety. For the first two laps of the race, Hector held his boat back to make sure his noble passenger didn't become alarmed, but in the final sprint for the finish line, with the wind in the perfect position for high speed, His Excellency became so caught up in the excitement that he stood and urged Hector to let the *Marinion* fly.

Hector obliged, and the governor general became the fastest viceroy in the world as both boats topped sixty miles per hour at the finish line. The governor general's iceboat ride received press coverage around the British Empire. Photographs of Earl Grey giving Hector a golden sovereign were printed in newspapers from Great Britain to Australia.

In honour of the occasion, Mr. McDonell was building a new boat, which he planned to name after the governor general's boss, King Edward VII. When it was finished, Tommy would inherit the *Marinion.*

Sitting beside Hector was Eddie Durnan, skipper of the *Britannia.* Eddie was a member of the famous Durnan family, which owned a big hotel at Gibraltar Point on the islands. A decade ago his family had donated a trophy known as the Durnan Cup. The cup race was held near the end of February just before the harbour thawed and the season officially ended. Durnan's trophy was considered the top racing prize of the year, but Eddie had yet to win it, mostly thanks to Fred and Hector. Beside Eddie was Joe Goodwin, skipper of the *Zoraya*; Bung Mullaney, skipper of the *Jack Frost*; and James Quinn, skipper of the *Alexandria*. The *Eel King* was skippered by Ed Gooch, and Jack Humphrey helmed the *Seneca*.

Despite being new, I was made to feel right at home by the older men. When Tommy mentioned I had already fallen off the boat, they said I had been officially baptized. Lulled by the warm fire and the accordion music, I almost dozed off until Ed poked me.

"We'd run you home," Tommy said, "but the wind's gone."

I nodded. "It's not that far. I'll see you soon."

4

# Ice Takes No Prisoners

## January 1, 1907

My second sailing lesson was the next school holiday, New Year's Day. Fred Phelan and Bung Mullaney were checking out the *IT*. I waved to them as I skidded across the ice toward the *Marinion*. A tall boat with a Union Jack at the top of its yard blocked my path. It was the Toronto police iceboat. Cork floats and safety ropes were mounted on special hooks on both ends of the boat. Mostly, the boat was for saving people who went through the ice. Occasionally, though, the police chased and arrested an iceboat skipper for "furious driving." Although there was no stated speed limit on the bay, ice boats were expected to slow down as they approached the crowded ice near the city.

I recognized a familiar face on the Harbour Police boat. Worse, the face recognized me — it was Jack, the policeman who had held me by the collar in the market on Christmas Eve.

"McCross? Is that you again?"

"Yes, Constable," I answered, feeling my blood run cold. I wasn't sure whether the bay was part of my out-of-bounds.

"Staying out of trouble?"

"Yes, sir."

"Good. Don't make me put you in our ice jail," the bull said, pointing at the shore. When I looked, the cops, Tommy, and Ed fell over laughing.

"Good one, Jack," Tommy said.

"What a carp," Ed agreed, making the motions of reeling me in. "Hook, line, and sinker."

I laughed, too, more out of relief than humour. If the bull was making jokes with me, that meant I was allowed to be here.

There was still so much to learn. Besides ropes and sailing orders, I had to figure out how to read ice. For non-sailors all ice seemed the same, but as soon as you sailed on it, you knew different. From shore the ice appeared as solid as land, but bay ice was actually like a jigsaw puzzle made up of huge floating pieces that were constantly moving. The wind and water currents separated and jammed the pieces together. Sometimes the slabs broke apart with a loud creak, revealing open water ranging from a few inches to a gap big enough to swallow an entire boat.

Other times two or more big slabs of ice slammed together, and the place where they met bulged up like a small mountain range. Iceboats either went around these or tried to go over them.

"The little ones aren't too bad," Ed told me, "but I once saw Fred Phelan fly over one that must have been six feet high."

"What happened?" I asked.

Tommy smiled. "He went flying like a kite for about

a hundred feet and then landed stern first with a crash. His boat just shattered like matchsticks, and there was Fred sitting on the ice surrounded by half a ton of kindling and belly-laughing like a maniac."

"The two crew members who were with him didn't think it was so funny, though," Ed said from the port outrigger. "One broke his arm and the other couldn't sit down without a feather cushion under his tailbone for a month."

On really cold days when the wind was blowing, the ice "talked" to you. Sometimes, without warning, it just went *boom!* like a cannon. At first that made me nearly jump out of my boots, and Tommy and Ed laughed their heads off. Other times the ice rang like a bell.

"That's the ice maids saying, 'Dinner's coming!'" Ed told me the first time that happened.

"What do ice maids eat for dinner?" I asked.

"Iceboats."

Another hazard I learned about were the ice men, and these guys were real. Ice men made their living by taking ice out of the bay in the winter, storing it in huge warehouses full of sawdust, and selling it by the block in the summer. As soon as the bay froze over, they drove huge horse-drawn wagons out onto the ice. Then, with a horse and blade or long, sharp saws, they took out ice in big rectangular blocks. In a typical day a team of ice men could make a hole big enough to drop a house through. Overnight, cold air would freeze the surface, but for a few days the ice over the hole would be very thin. After a light sprinkling of snow, such holes turned into perfect traps for unwary iceboats or skaters.

Most of the ice men were considerate and marked the holes in the ice with rag flags or abandoned Christmas trees. Unfortunately, some lazy louts left their ice holes unmarked, and nearly every year someone fell through a hole. Fortunately, Tommy knew where most of the bad ice men operated. "Down by the Yonge Street sewer," he told me.

"What?"

"They're too lazy to go too far out on the ice, so they get their ice where the Yonge Street sewer empties into the bay. Remember that the next time your mom's buying ice for your afternoon lemonade."

The lemonade crack was another joke in a running theme Tommy and Ed had recently invented. Lemonade was a "posh" drink, and to them I was a posh or rich kid despite the fact that my family was as dead broke as theirs.

"Posh isn't just money in the bank," Ed said. "You talk posh and you dress posh."

I knew by dressing posh they meant that my clothes weren't hand-me-downs with patches. Yet.

"How does one talk posh?" I asked.

"How does one talk posh?" Ed mimicked, and both he and Tommy whooped with laughter.

I knew they were just kidding me, so I didn't mind too much. Whenever I said something that sounded posh to them, they called me Lord Simcoe, after Ontario's first lieutenant governor, though the province was called Upper Canada then. When I told them Simcoe was never a lord, they just laughed harder.

"Only a Lord Simcoe would know that," Ed would say.

There was no way to win.

Despite the kidding, Tommy and Ed were great friends to me. When we picked up a paying fare, they now split the money three ways, even though I was still barely better than self-moving ballast. We snagged three fares on New Year's morning, and I had to admit that I enjoyed showing off a little for a pair of young ladies who had hired us for an around-the-harbour tour. That Simon guy had been right. You did see some nice views on this job, and a glimpse of a well-turned ankle made nearly almost any guy show off a bit.

With the ladies aboard we were running fast with a steady south wind on our starboard as we crossed from the Western Gap to the Eastern Gap. Ed and I were leaning out a bit on the runner when a fluke gust made the boat hike without warning. I had been enjoying the admiring look the shop girls were giving Ed and me, so I wasn't thinking about what I was doing. When the runner hiked, I fell off and went spinning across the ice without a boat.

"Man overboard!" Ed yelled.

"Man overboard!" Tommy echoed, dropping sail and turning the tiller hard so that the *Marinion* cut sharply around.

"Is the kid all right?" one of the two shop girls cried.

*Kid?* I thought as I bounced across the ice.

"Are you all right, Your Lordship?" Ed asked as they cruised to a halt beside me. "Anything hurt?"

"Just my pride," I said, rubbing my sore bum.

"Funny place for your pride," Ed commented.

When the shop girls sniggered, I turned red.

"Gotta watch for flukes, Simcoe," Tommy said. "This is no place for daydreaming, and make sure you keep both hands on the ropes at all times."

"Aye, aye, Captain," I said as Ed and I pushed the *Marinion* into the wind and we began sailing again. It wasn't long before I found out that a sore bum wasn't the worse thing ice can give you.

The next day we came across a group of people standing in a wide circle just off Mugg's Landing near the Western Gap. A dog had fallen through an ice hole, and its owners were helpless to save it. It was a huge mutt, a Newfoundland with maybe some Bernese or St. Bernard thrown in somewhere, but even with all that power it couldn't get out on its own.

"C'mon, boy!" people shouted. "C'mon!"

But every time the dog got a paw on the ice, it broke and the mutt plunged in again.

"Look at him shivering," Ed said. "He hasn't much left."

"Two minutes more at best, I'd say," Tommy said. "Simcoe, you're the lightest."

"What? You want me to walk out there and get him?"

"No. All you have to do is lie on your stomach. We'll do the rest."

Tommy told me that we were going to form a human chain with me as the last link. I didn't want any part of this deal, but one look at that doomed dog and my body started moving toward the hole against my will. "Okay, okay, I'm going."

"Not too close, Bertie," Tommy said. "Lie down now."

I dropped first to my knees, then to my belly. I felt Ed's powerful hands grip my ankles as he slowly pushed me toward the hole. From this angle I could barely see the dog. Only the tip of its nose stuck above the ice, and occasionally a massive paw rose up and frantically clawed for a foothold.

"Hold on, boy, we're coming for you," I said as Tommy pushed Ed and me forward. Then I heard the ice crack beneath me and I stopped.

"Relax, Simcoe," Ed said. "You're still okay."

Another man was now pushing Tommy forward. The cracking grew louder, and suddenly I knew I was sinking. The ice was fracturing all around me like a spiderweb. I was so frightened that I figured my heart was going to hammer a hole through the ice. Frigid water welled up from the cracks in the ice underneath me, burning like fire as it seeped through my clothes and touched my skin.

"Maybe we should quit," Ed said when he saw how deep I was sinking.

It was my call, but I was so close that I thought I could feel the dog's breath on my hand. "Just push me out a little farther," I urged, and Ed slid me another foot forward. The ice continued to crack and the water soaked my chest, but I was able to thrust my hands over the rim of the hole. "C'mon, boy!" I called. "C'mon!" Still no answer.

"He's gone!" someone yelled from the shore.

I refused to believe it. I called and whistled for another full minute before Ed and Tommy reluctantly pulled me in. As soon as I stood, the wind hit me in my wet clothes and I began to shiver. Someone threw a horse blanket around me.

"Get him somewhere warm fast," another man said.

The rest of the day was spent sitting in an ice-fishing hut watching two old guys haul in perch and pickerel while clouds of steam rose from my clothes as they hung on a line over a small wood stove. I didn't dare go home soaking wet or else I'd never be allowed to sail again.

I felt very depressed about not saving the dog. Jack, the harbour cop, stopped by with a glass jar of oxtail soup for me and guessed what I was thinking.

"Don't be so hard on yourself, McCross. That happens to us all the time. A dog is bad enough, but imagine what it's like when it's a person in the water. Especially a kid like you. You do your best, but sometimes Lady Luck just says no."

Tommy and Ed returned at dusk to take me home.

"Here, I made these for you," Ed said, handing me a strange gift. "Pray you never have to use them." It looked like a skipping rope with a pair of wooden pegs on each end connected by a three-foot-long piece of strong twine. Each peg had a cap on the bottom which, when removed, displayed a half-inch nail.

"Thanks," I said. "What the heck are they?"

"Picks," Ed said. "Your ticket out of an ice hole."

"What?"

"They go through your jacket arms like mittens, one down each sleeve so you can always reach them without looking," Ed explained, shaking both of his arms so that two picks fell out. "If you go through the ice, you'll never pull yourself out with your bare hands. The ice is too slippery and your clothes will pull you down. Use these picks like claws. Shake off the caps and stab each pick into the ice. If you can't pull yourself out, hang on until someone reaches you."

That night, for the first time in years, I cried myself to sleep. It started with remembering that poor dog in the ice. Then I thought about my father losing his job and my mother's rough hands as she struggled to cope with being poor. Now we lived in a rented house stinking of rendered animal carcasses and laundry bleach. We hadn't done anything bad to deserve this. We did our best, but sometimes Lady Luck just said no.

5

# The Russell

## January 6, 1907

Even though he had been up all night, this morning Father accompanied me to York Street to meet Tommy and Ed and see the *Marinion* for himself. There were about twenty boats parked on the ice already. A couple of minor races were scheduled for the afternoon, but the big "event" of the day was a contest between Fred Phelan's new iceboat *IT* and a motor car.

The race was a publicity stunt organized by Thomas Russell, general manager of the Canadian Cycle and Motor Company, more commonly known as CCM. These days CCM was one of the biggest bicycle manufacturers in the British Empire, but Russell had saved the company from near bankruptcy at the turn of the century by introducing ice skates and hockey equipment to its inventory so that the firm had something to produce and sell in winter when bicycles were put away. Now Russell was toying with a new-fangled contraption — the Russell, an automobile he had named after himself.

"Hi, Tommy!" I said as we slid down the lake embankment. "Hey, Ed!"

"Whoops! Whoops!" my father cried, almost falling on his face as his feet touched the ice.

"Watch it there, sir," Tommy warned, grabbing Father by the arm to steady him.

"Thank you," my father said, regaining his balance. "I believe I've worn entirely improper foot attire for this activity."

Ed glanced at Father's perfectly polished brogues and said in a mock-British accent, "Egad, sir, I do believe you have." Then he switched back to his normal voice. "Easy to see where you get your posh talk, Bertie."

"Next time try wearing something with treads, Mr. McCross, and save your fine leather for the office," Tommy suggested.

It was a perfect morning for racing. The last few days of rain and high winds had polished the bay ice mirror-smooth. Today the sun was shining and a stiff and steady fifteen-mile-per-hour wind gusted from the west. The boats would have the wind abeam for at least two legs of the race, which meant running times would be fast.

Tommy skipped the first race so we could give Father a decent ride. "My, my goodness!" he exclaimed as we shot like a bullet down Blockhouse Bay toward Mugg's Landing. The shoreline was coming up quickly. I was proud that Father didn't scream or show the least bit of fear as Tommy leaned on the tiller and the *Marinion* swung hard to starboard. We shot back out through the Long Pond gap even faster than we had come in.

Out on the bay the wind caused the port runner blade to bounce like a racehorse impatiently stamping its hoof. Ed and I gripped the shroud wires, stood, and eased out onto the beam to add weight to the port side. Father said nothing, but his jaw hung open as we increased speed. I could tell he was frightened — not for himself but for me. I tried to reassure him by smiling and giving him a thumb's up.

Bad mistake. At just that moment our starboard runner nicked a pressure crack and the boat heeled sharply to the right. Because I was holding on with one hand, the sudden change of direction threw me off the beam like a sack of flour. I landed on my back and hurtled across the ice at nearly forty miles per hour. At that speed I realized why iceboating was called "hard water sailing." I could feel every bump and ridge as I skidded along like an overturned turtle.

"Are you all right?" Tommy asked even before I came to a stop. He had dropped the mainsail and swung around. My bottom felt as if it were on fire, and I was so dizzy from the spinning that I was afraid I'd throw up if I moved.

"Bertie!" my father called out fearfully.

I knew if I appeared the least bit hurt, my sailing days were over. My body took over, and I began to quiver.

"Is he hurt?" Ed asked.

"Is he crying?" Tommy added.

"No," Father said with relief. "He's laughing."

Father was right. My lungs exploded in the biggest belly laugh I had ever experienced. "That … was … amazing!" I sputtered between bouts of laughter.

Then the laughter became infectious, and Tommy and Ed started snorting, too.

"You … should … have … seen … you ... standing there … with that big, stupid … grin … and then *bump!*

You're gone," Tommy cackled.

"I looked ... and there you were ... gone!" Ed wheezed.

Even my father began to laugh. "How do you feel, Bertie?

"Fine," I said, finally able to stand and dust myself off. "But my bum hurts."

"Looks like they're getting ready for the second race," Ed said. "We'd better get back if we want to enter."

Father stood on the shore as we lined up for the second heat. Today, to accommodate the *IT*/Russell match, the races were starting down by the Western Gap where more spectators could watch. In our race we stood a pretty good chance against the older boats *Reindeer, Snow Queen, Island Girl, Snow Drift*, and *Idler*. The guys to beat, though, were Ed Durnan in the *Britannia* and John Hanlan in the *Vigilant*.

The starting pistol barked, and all eight crews scrambled to push their boats forward while their skippers hauled hard on the halyards to raise sail. *Reindeer* grabbed an early lead, but its skipper allowed Durnan to steal his wind with *Britannia*'s larger sail. Tommy kept *Marinion* just off *Vigilant*'s port runner. With the wind blowing strong on our starboard beam, it took less than a minute before the first boats turned hard around the first post and steered for York Street.

*Britannia* and *Vigilant* made the corner smartly. Tommy had to swing wide to avoid hitting *Snow Drift*, which lived up to its name by stalling on the turn and causing *Island Girl* and *Idler* to tangle sails and rigging to avoid colliding with it. By the time we reached the curve, *Britannia* and *Vigilant* were a hundred and fifty yards ahead of us, but we were closing rapidly. Durnan and Hanlan rounded the York post and turned into the wind for the Western Gap leg.

Now it was a sailors' race as each captain and crew had to tack back and forth against the wind. *Britannia* and *Vigilant* looked like a ballet team as they zigzagged across the ice in perfect unison. Tommy noticed that both Durnan and Hanlan were encountering rippled ice called "washboard," which slowed their boats down. So he swung wide to make up time on the smoother ice along the north shore. This tactic gave us a lot less room to manoeuvre. To make sure we didn't hit the shore or the washboard, we had to change tack every fifteen seconds. With each swing of the boat, Ed and I had to scuttle back and forth along the runner beam like squirrels, but we were gaining.

As the *Britannia* and *Vigilant* bounced across the washboard, we narrowed the gap between them and us rapidly. We caught the two lead boats just as they broke free of the washboard. Now it was a three-way heat for the last hundred yards to the finish line.

Then I was startled by a loud roar. About five hundred people had lined the shore to cheer us on.

"Where did they come from?" I hollered to Ed as we crouched low to offer minimum wind resistance. Hanlan and Durnan were inching closer on either side of us. Then the long prow of the *Britannia* began to push in front. The noise from the onshore crowd continued to rise as *Vigilant* edged in front of us.

It looked as if we were in for a third-place finish when suddenly the *Britannia*'s left runner threw its blade and the huge boat lurched heavily to port, throwing two of its crewmen onto the ice. Both Tommy and John Hanlan dropped sails and veered to starboard to avoid hitting skidding sailors shooting across our bows like ice porpoises.

Although the *Vigilant* had technically won the race, Hanlan voluntarily split the prize money evenly with us because both boats had to cut speed to avoid running over the *Britannia*'s crew. The *Reindeer* came in third despite a broken bowsprit. A big cheer went up as the remaining boats all limped in — finishing a race under one's own power was considered an accomplishment.

Of course, most of the crowd on the shore wasn't there to see us. For weeks the newspapers had attempted to outdo one another by building up enthusiasm for the *IT*/Russell race. As skipper of the fastest iceboat in Toronto, Fred Phelan was already a local celebrity. His photo appeared in the papers nearly every week, and several articles had been written about his racing exploits and fearless sailing.

Thomas Russell's face was also well known to the public. The *IT*/Russell race was the latest in a series of sporting events he had organized pitting his cars against champion bicyclists, racehorses, and even express trains. Once just expensive toys, horseless carriages had come a long way in the past few years.

CCM had already experimented with small electric motor buggies and a steam-powered car called the Locomobile, but these had failed to capture the public's attention or, more important, their wallets. The electric car could only be driven a few dozen miles before it needed recharging, and the steam car was notorious for breaking down. People called it the No-Go Mobile. Gas-powered automobiles were more reliable and had better range, but most people were afraid of them because of the noise and smoke they produced. Albert Pope, an American electric car manufacturer, summed it up best when he said: "No sensible person would voluntarily sit over an explosion."

In spite of that attitude, Russell had somehow convinced the CCM board of directors to let him manufacture gasoline-powered automobiles. In 1905 the Russell Model A first appeared on Toronto streets. A larger, more powerful Model B was unveiled a few months later. In 1906 Models C and D were released.

Russell wasn't the sort of man who avoided risks. When his latest automobile, the Model E, appeared in the CCM showroom before the year was finished, he confidently declared to the newspapers that it could beat an iceboat — even the *IT* skipped by Fred Phelan. After Phelan was informed of Russell's boast, his face lit up in a wide grin.

"Well," he said at the time as he raised the sail on the *IT*, "if Mr. Russell wants to race, he knows where to find me." That day Fred's *IT* clocked eighty-eight miles per hour on a fast run between the Eastern and Western Gaps. When given this information, Russell said, "That's in one direction with a favourable wind. My car will go fifty miles per hour in any direction with any wind. Tell Mr. Phelan the race is on."

Over the past few weeks several journalists had been given test rides in a Russell at a horse track to show off its racing abilities. These trips, however, had been on dry land and in a Model D with just an eighteen-horsepower, two-cylinder engine. The Model E was equipped with a twenty-five-horsepower, four-cylinder engine. No one knew how fast this newest version could go. There were rumours that Russell had personally test-driven his new car on Lake Couchiching, just north of Toronto, but he had refused to reveal the outcome. As a result, the racing bookies were completely in the dark about what odds to offer. Three weeks before the match the *IT* was given two-to-one odds. The next week, after good write-ups by some car-converted journalists, the Russell was awarded three-to-two odds. Then Phelan won three races out of four against two visiting boats from Windsor, and the odds became dead even.

Now a shady-looking guy in a checkered overcoat called out, "Last chance for bets! One for one!" Three men, including one of the harbour policemen, placed last-minute wagers — all on the Russell.

Tommy fingered the dollar he had won. "We really should support Fred."

Ed agreed. He, too, took out his dollar.

I felt a tug, as well, but there was no way I could gamble, especially with my father standing beside me.

Just then an unbelievable racket made everyone gawk at the shoreline. Blasts of black smoke snorted up from behind the wall of spectators. The accompanying noise sounded like thunder mixed with rattling swords and something akin to geese honking. The mob parted slightly to let a large black metallic object lumber through like a prowling bear. Tommy and Ed put their dollars back in their pockets.

Five men sat in the car, two in front, three in back. The driver, sitting at the front right, paused only for a split second at the top of the embankment before he fearlessly slid the car down the steep grade that led to the ice.

"Who the heck would ever want to own one of those?" I asked my father as we felt the ice shudder when the front wheels hit the frozen lake. He nodded, but I don't think he heard me, and I noticed that his eyes weren't tearing for once. Instead they were shining like a man smitten. Only an engineer could love a contraption like that, I thought.

"That crate's going right through the ice," Ed said, clamping his hands over his ears.

Russell's final touch of genius was that he promised not to enter a specially modified racing version of his car for the event. Up against Phelan's champion boat *IT*, Russell was running a standard family vehicle picked at random from his showroom by a reporter. For safety the car had been stripped of doors, windshield, and anything else that might prevent a fast exit for the crew in case the contraption went through the ice. Everything else, though, was standard Russell.

A man in a top hat and expensive coat climbed out of the passenger seat at the left front of the car. From his photographs in the newspaper, I knew it was Thomas Russell himself. One of the three men in the back of the automobile took Russell's place in the front.

The four CCM employees wore identical black bowler hats, which my father said were good head protection. "They were created fifty years ago for the second Earl of Leicester as crash helmets for people riding horses," he told me. "The round crown on top is crash-resistant, and the stiff brim all the way round protects the head from a lateral fall. In France they call the hat a *chapeau melon* because it makes an Englishman's head look like a melon."

"Well, I'm sure Fred won't have any trouble beating these melon heads," Tommy said as the four men sat like statues while newspaper photographers blasted away, their powder flashes adding to the excitement.

"Yes —" I was about to agree, but the words froze in my mouth. For a moment I thought I had seen a blaze of red hair and freckles watching me from the shoreline, but when I looked again they were gone. I told myself I was imagining things.

Russell knew how to play to a crowd. He raised his top hat to the spectators, then made a sweeping gesture to his car and driving team. In unison the four men raised their bowler hats with their right hands in salute. The spectators went wild. Russell gave each man in his crew a big cigar.

As if on cue, Phelan now approached from York Street, the *IT* gracefully sweeping from port to starboard. In response the driver of the Russell cranked the throttle mounted on the steering wheel up and down, and the engine revved in several snarling blasts. Clouds of rank black smoke rolled across the lake like fog, and people coughed. Frowning, Russell made a throat-slashing motion to the driver, and the man instantly cut the engine. The car manufacturer smiled and bowed to the crowd again.

"Can you imagine what this city would be like if everyone owned one of those monsters?" Ed asked, holding his nose. "We'd all die from ass ... ass-fixya."

"Those things cost fifteen years' wages for stiffs like us," Tommy said. "They'll never be anything more than just noisy nuisances."

When the *IT* came to a rest, Phelan climbed off to shake hands with Russell and the driver of the car. The crowd applauded, whistled, and stamped on the wooden boards they had brought to keep their feet warm.

The rules were simple. The racecourse was shaped like a triangle, with a total length of seven miles per circuit. They racers had to go twice around. The first vehicle over the finish line won a hundred dollars. For safety the police ordered almost everyone up on the frozen shoreline but, as racers, we were allowed to stay on the ice.

"C'mon, let's get comfortable," Tommy said, pulling the *Marinion* around so we could sit on it as if it were a park bench. Ed had even packed some fried baloney sandwiches, his favourite food.

"A true genius," my father said of Russell as a throng of reporters peppered him with questions. "For just a hundred-dollar prize he's getting a thousand dollars' worth of advertising."

"You'd think he was giving away free turkeys," Tommy muttered with a mouthful of baloney.

"Hey, we need a couple of strong backs here!" Phelan called to Tommy and Ed.

They dropped their sandwiches and ran out to help him move the *IT* to the starting line. With a nod from Russell, one of his crew ran around to the front of the car with a steel crank in hand. He inserted the device and gave it a couple of hard turns. The engine sputtered and died. The driver made an adjustment on the throttle and told his teammate to turn the crank again. This time the engine caught with a hellish roar, and the Russell chugged up to take its place beside the *IT*. For this race Phelan was sailing with only one crewman, but Tommy and Ed were allowed to help push them off when the contest began because the Russell had four men aboard.

One of the Harbour Patrol bulls took a revolver out of a locked chest on his iceboat and walked over to the starting line. He looked at Russell, who nodded, then the constable pointed the pistol in the air, counted to three, and fired. The gunshot was swallowed by the mighty roar that went up from the crowd. Tommy's and Ed's feet were blurs as the two boys gave the *IT* their hardest push. Phelan and his crewman jumped aboard and threw the sail into the wind as fast as they could. Nearby a spray of ice slivers shot out from the Russell's back wheels as the driver hammered the car's throttle down full with his fist. With the wind abeam, Phelan and the *IT* took off like a greyhound, while the Russell spun its wheels and fishtailed right and left as the driver struggled to get traction.

"Look at Fred go!" Tommy shouted as he and Ed resumed their seats on the *Marinion*.

It was about two miles to the first post, and Phelan made it there in under two minutes, but the Russell, once it got up to speed, was moving very fast and was narrowing the lead. At the Eastern Gap turn the *IT*'s blades bit firmly into the ice and swung smartly around the marker, Phelan and his crewman ducking gracefully as the boom swung over their heads. The sail caught the breeze with a snap, and the *IT* accelerated again.

The Russell, on the other hand, went into a lumbering skid when its driver tried to turn. Rooster tails of ice flew up from the rear wheels, and the engine bellowed like an enraged buffalo as the car clawed the ice, trying to regain forward momentum. Again the Russell picked up speed, but Phelan's iceboat was so far ahead it looked as if the race was already over.

I almost felt sorry for Russell, whose shoulders seemed to sag as he watched Phelan's *IT* make a fool out of his namesake.

"Would you care for a seat, Mr. Russell?" Tommy asked, perhaps thinking the same thing I was.

Russell turned and saw Tommy patting a stretch of deck between himself and my father. "Why ... yes, thank you," the CCM bigwig said with genuine appreciation.

That was the great thing about Tommy. He could talk to anyone and make him feel instantly at home.

"Sandwich?" Ed asked, offering Russell a lunch bucket full of baloney sandwiches with hot mustard and dill pickles.

Russell licked his lips and accepted a sandwich. "Thanks. Missed my breakfast."

"Looks like you've got a real race, sir," my father said, smiling. He dabbed his eyes with his handkerchief, but so were a lot of people due to the bright sun and lake wind.

"I fear I may have bitten off a little more than I can chew," Russell said. "And I don't mean this fine sandwich."

"Your automobile's definitely at a disadvantage on two out of three legs of this race," my father admitted, "but the third leg could prove interesting when the *IT* turns into the wind."

Just as my father said that, the *IT* rounded the second marker and began the final leg of the first lap. As he had predicted, the Russell closed the distance fast as Phelan was forced to tack back and forth in a wide zigzag after the automobile rounded the second post, recovered from its skid, and made straight for the third. Like Tommy, Phelan had chosen to avoid the washboard and swing wide to the smooth ice on the outside. The Russell drove straight up the inside, the washboard causing the machine to shake violently as it flew over the ice. A lesser driver would have slowed down or lost control, but Russell had chosen his man well. The driver fearlessly poured on the speed. Bouncing in unison, his three passengers clenched their cigars in their teeth and clung to whatever they could grab on the automobile.

The *IT* and the Russell rounded the third post almost simultaneously. From where we sat on the *Marinion*, it seemed as if they were about to collide, but somehow they missed each other as the *IT* turned hard to port while the Russell shot past like a charging bull.

"Come on, Fred!" Tommy yelled.

"Fine driving, Jones!" Russell shouted.

"It's going to be very close," my father said to Russell.

"How can you tell?" Tommy asked.

"Both men know their machines. Each has an advantage over the other. The *IT* can outrun the Russell when the wind's abeam, but on the third leg the Russell can travel in a straight line when Phelan's forced to tack. It's going to be a question of whether Phelan can build up enough of a lead on the first two legs or whether Jones can close that lead and take it in the final dash."

"Jones is the best driver in the country," Russell said. "I found him in South Carolina testing steam cars on the beach during low tide. Unofficially, he's clocked higher than a hundred miles per hour on packed sand."

"Interesting men, these iceboats sailors," my father said. "But they're still living in the nineteenth century."

"What do you mean ... Mr. ...?" Russell asked, extending his hand.

"McCross," my father said. "At your service, sir." He took Russell's hand and shook it, then continued his lecture.

"Their boats are still all wood frames with iron fittings, canvas sails, and hemp rigging. These craft are virtually identical to iceboats that were sailing in the time of Admiral Nelson. Imagine how much faster an iceboat could go if it was constructed out of modern materials like bicycle-frame tube steel and carbon-steel skate blades. A silk sail would weigh less than a tenth of a canvas one."

Russell laughed. "I'm glad you weren't building the *IT*." He was nodding enthusiastically with every suggestion my father made. "Are you an engineer?"

"I am."

"Where do you work?"

"I ... I'm self-employed," my father said.

A sudden cheer brought their attention back to the race. Phelan had managed to widen the lead in the second lap. Each time the Russell turned, the rear end of the machine swung out and the car skidded dangerously. Twice it almost flipped over, but the two CCM crew on the passengers' side imitated Phelan's mate by climbing out onto the car's inside running board and leaned into the turn, which earned thunderous applause from the spectators on the shore. But the CCM men's efforts still weren't good enough.

As Phelan rounded the third post for the final time, it was clear that the *IT* had a commanding lead that even a superb driver like Jones had no hope of overcoming. But Jones kept racing. He whipped the Russell around the third post at full throttle even as Phelan was already halfway home. The Russell bucked like a horse as Jones threw it across the washboard with no thought of giving up. Just three more short tacks and Phelan would be over the finish line.

Russell continued to smile, but it was a bit forced now. He was being a good sport, but we could tell he was disappointed.

*"Go! Go! Go! Go! Go! Go! Go! Go!"* the people along the shoreline shouted, but it was impossible to tell whether they were rooting for the Russell or for the *IT*. Half the bookies seemed delighted, while the other half looked ready to chop a hole in the ice and dive through it. For the non-bettors the outcome didn't matter. They had come to see a spectacular race, and they were certainly getting that.

Suddenly, Tommy, Ed, and a few of the other boat skippers stood and gazed at the sky.

"What's wrong?" I yelled over the screaming crowd.

"Wind's changing," Tommy said. "It's dying!"

The landlubbers on the shore didn't notice anything, but we could see Phelan and his first mate glance at each other in the middle of their third and final tack. Then their sail sagged and the boom slackened against the sheet. The mate said something to Phelan, which might have been an offer to get out and push, but the skipper shook his head. In Toronto there was an unwritten iceboating rule that didn't allow craft to be pushed over the finish line. They had to finish under sail. Phelan would rather lose a race than be accused of bending the rules.

The *IT* slowed to a halt as the Russell thundered toward the finish line. Jones was oblivious to Phelan's troubles as he struggled to keep the car straight on the washboard.

"Holy Moly!" Ed cried as the Russell crossed the finish line still cranked at full throttle. Only then did Jones notice the steep, frozen embankment coming straight at him.

*Hssssssssssss!* went the car as Jones laid on the brakes and fought to keep the automobile from rolling when it corkscrewed. Bowler hats and cigars went flying in all directions as the Russell threw up snow and ice shards. The tires on the passenger side caught a snow ridge crack, and the vehicle violently reared up sideways on two wheels. It hung there for a few seconds before it fell back down heavily on all four wheels. Another cheer went up.

The crowd on the shore burst through the police line and poured onto the lake ice. Within seconds both the car and its crew was surrounded by thousands of cheering bodies.

"Congratulations, Mr. Russell," my father said, offering the CCM his hand. "You won your race."

"I did, but I was very fortunate, Mr. McCross," the CCM boss admitted. "Sometimes Lady Luck says yes, and there's no shame in it," he said over his shoulder as he marched toward the finish line where Phelan and the *IT* were creeping to a halt with Tommy and Ed pushing them.

Jones led his team forward to shake hands with Phelan and his crewman. Reporters shouted questions at Russell and the *IT*'s skipper, and several rival photographers jostled for the best spot to set up their cumbersome tripods to take pictures of the race's participants.

In the swirl of bodies on the ice, I lost track of my father. It was like walking through a human snowstorm. And then out of the blur, right in front of me, was Sean Kelly with his arms crossed. Hughie and Sonny were on either side of me. I didn't have to look to know I was blocked from behind.

Sean stepped forward with his fists clenched. I started to raise my arms, but suddenly the lights went out in broad daylight. Then someone grabbed my upper arms in a bear hug. At first I thought I had already been mercifully knocked out except that I could still hear people talking and moving about. What was Sean up to? Maybe he wanted to string the beating out to make me suffer even more.

For some reason my body didn't switch to automatic survival, so I had to use my brain to get out of the mess. I remembered leafing through one of father's books about Japanese hand-to-hand fighting techniques. Most of it was pretty unbelievable stuff, showing guys in crazy haircuts and baggy pants breaking bricks with their bare hands or fighting ten swordsmen with a broomstick, but I recalled one page where someone was held from behind exactly the way one of the Kellys had me. The solution was simple — stamp a heel on the guy's toes.

*"Ow-wow-wow!"* the Kelly screeched.

I had missed his toes, but my boot heel had barked six inches of skin off his shin. With my arms released I swung my fist in a wide arc and felt a satisfying smack as I connected with a Kelly chin. Then I reached up and grabbed whatever was covering my eyes. It was a bowler hat.

"Oh, my stars!" a voice said from the ice. It was Ed, holding his chin. Tommy was hopping about in circles on one leg.

"You guys beat the Kellys?" I demanded.

"What?" Tommy cried.

"The Kellys. They were right here. They had me trapped and you saved me."

"There weren't any Kellys, you moron," Ed said. "That was us. We put the hat over your head as a joke. Tommy grabbed you in case you tried to walk and bump into someone."

"No!" I insisted. "The Kellys were right here. Sean himself and about ten of his gang. I swear."

Even in their pain Tommy and Ed could see the humour of the situation. "Come to think of it," Ed said, "I did see a flash of freckles pass by before you slugged me with that haymaker. Then I saw stars."

"*Ow-wow-wow.* I'm going to be hobbling for a week." Tommy grimaced, then released one of his high-pitched horse whinnies. He picked the bowler off the ground and handed it to me brim side up. "We found this on the ice and decided you should have it because of the way you like to go iceboat sailing without an iceboat. How's the bum, by the way?"

"Well, we've all got something to remember today by," I said. "Your chin, your shin, and my — ah, hello, Father."

My father had just emerged from the crowd, carrying a small white card.

"What's that?" Tommy asked.

"Mr. Russell's business card," Father said. "When we were talking to the CMM crew, Mr. Russell kept asking me questions about what I thought about his motor car. I didn't know it, but I think he was testing my knowledge. Just before he left he said that if I was ever looking for a job, they were looking for engineers."

"Are you going to call?" I asked.

Father paused and thought hard. "I don't know, son." He dabbed his eyes. "I still have a lot of books to read."

6

# The Albatross

## January 12, 1907

After the mobs of people who watched the *IT*/Russell race, Toronto's harbour seemed almost deserted by comparison when I showed up for sailing the following Saturday. Saturdays generally drew a noisier, more rambunctious crowd than the Sundays when we got most of our family business. Our usual Saturday fares were shop clerks, factory workers, and trade apprentices from the nearby factories and warehouses.

After two hours of constant running to the islands and back, we stopped for some tea at the iceboat anchorage at York Street. Tommy and Ed went over to talk to Hector about next week's racing schedule.

I was sitting on the *Marinion* absentmindedly pretending to steer the tiller when a female voice behind me said, "I see you've abandoned tree climbing for ice sailing."

When I turned, there, five feet away, was a beautiful young lady in an expensive winter coat, fur-trimmed gloves, and matching boots. Beneath her matching fur hat was a fringe of reddish-gold hair that had a mind of its own. She seemed vaguely familiar. The tree remark rebounded through my brain and then it came to me — it was the girl I'd seen in the market standing next to a suit of armour.

"Oh, hello," I ventured. "Did you enjoy your Christmas truffles?"

The girl's instant smile filled my veins with soda bubbles. "Oh, you remember me," she said, hopping up and down on the ice.

"You remembered me from my tree-climbing days," I said.

"It was easier. Except for the bowler hat, you're still wearing the same clothes."

Her remark hit me like a slap in the face, and my embarrassment must have been visible.

"Oh, I'm sorry. I didn't mean it like that. I mean, I'm wearing a completely different outfit today than I was then. I think I'd be much harder to recognize than —"

"Someone who hasn't changed his clothes in three weeks?" I suggested coldly.

"Oh, I'm sure you have other clothes —" the young lady began.

"Actually, no, I don't."

The girl flushed and looked as if she were about to run back up to Front Street. I felt like a prize idiot and wondered why I was trying to make her feel bad when I wanted her to stay ... a lot.

"One thing about it," I finally said. "It saves having to decide what you're going to wear in the morning." Fortunately, she recognized that as an attempt at a joke. I smiled. She smiled.

"I'd like to purchase a ride, please," she said. "Could you arrange that?" She smiled again. "By the way, my name is Isobel."

I was pretty sure I had a stupid grin plastered on my mug. "I sure could." I ran over to where Tommy and Ed were gassing with Hector and a few other boat skippers. "Hey, Tommy, we've got a customer."

Tommy made a wry face. "Aw, we were just going to have lunch. Tell those noisy factory dolts to find another boat."

Ed saw Isobel standing beside the boat. "Tom, I think you'll want this fare."

"Unless the governor general's back, I don't —" he began as he turned. Then he froze. Isobel waved, and I felt a pang of jealousy from the way Tommy said, "Wow!"

"Hello, my name is Isobel," she told Tommy and Ed, taking off her leather glove and offering a hand to Tommy.

He glanced at the hand with puzzlement. Behind her back I motioned to Tommy to take it. He did, but then hung on to it as if it were connected to a museum mummy. I gestured for him to shake it. Finally catching on, Tommy pumped Isobel's hand vigorously. I knew he was imitating the way the governor general had shaken hands with his father when all the press photographers were around. I half expected him to take off his hat and shout, *"Huzza!"* But now he was shaking her hand too long. I motioned for him to let go, and he finally did.

"How much is a ride?" Isobel asked, flexing the blood back into her hand.

Her question made Tommy relax. He was back on

familiar ground. “A dollar will get you a one-hour trip around the bay. Twenty-five cents will get you a one-way to the island, and the ride’s free if we don’t make it in less than a minute.”

“Less than a minute?” Isobel’s eyes shone. “You can make this boat go that fast?”

Tommy shrugged, completely confident. “With a decent breeze like today? Sure. Do it all the time.”

“Very well,” Isobel said, unpinning a small watch from the inside of her coat. “I shall time you.”

Ed and Tommy exchanged looks and laughed. “Don’t believe me, huh?” Tommy said.

“Men tend to exaggerate about most things,” Isobel said as if male overstatement were a proven fact. She put one dainty foot up on the cockpit. “Where do I stand?”

“You sit,” Tommy said sternly. “Right there, miss. Out of the way. Ed, Simcoe, let’s go. Twenty-five cents will buy us each a baked bean sandwich at Martha’s Open Kitchen.”

I winced. The great thing about Tommy was that he shared the money we earned, but I wished he didn’t also share our poor-people eating habits with our current passenger. With Isobel sitting securely in the cockpit, the three of us picked up the stern and swung the *Marinion* around to face the nearest shore of the islands. A brisk breeze blowing from the east promised a good run.

“Ready with your watch?” Tommy asked Isobel. “Say when!”

Flushed with excitement, Isobel waited for the second hand to cross the twelve on the dial face. “Ready ... go!” she cried.

*I'm finally getting the hang of this,* I thought as Tommy, Ed, and I kicked off together like a matched team of horses. At exactly the same time Ed and I swung up onto the runner beam while Tommy jumped onto the stern. The stiff wind filled our sail with a satisfying crack of canvas, and we felt the *Marinion* accelerate like a rocket under our feet. This was the moment I loved best. Even Ed and Tommy always seemed as if they were enjoying the thrill for the first time.

Isobel, tucked into the cockpit, let out a whoop of joy. *"Whoooeeeeeeeeee!"* she shrieked like a police siren, bringing a hockey game to a complete halt as the players gawked at us streaking by.

Despite her age, in this wind the *Marinion* ran like a young colt. Already the centre island was getting close.

"Thirty seconds!" Isobel called out, but we were already more than halfway there.

We were still accelerating when Tommy let the wind out of the sail and cranked the tiller so that it dragged the stern runner like a brake. If he hadn't done that, we would have gone up the bank and halfway across the island before we stopped. With an expert flourish he brought us to a dead stop and facing north back toward the city.

"Toronto Islands, as you requested, ma'am," he said.

"Forty-nine seconds." Isobel snapped her watch shut and reached for the change purse in her handbag.

"Just one question," Tommy said. "Exactly how do you plan to get back? We offer a round trip for thirty-five cents."

"Oh, I don't want to go back just yet," Isobel said. From her coat pocket she unfolded a large dollar note and handed it to Tommy.

He glanced at the bill, and his face broke into a grin. "Forget the beans, boys," he said to Ed and me. "We're eating corned beef for lunch."

I winced.

"Where to, m'lady?" Tommy asked.

"Go out as far and as fast as we can."

"The ice gets rough as we move out of the bay," Tommy warned.

"That sounds fine," Isobel said. "Take us there, please."

Tommy shrugged knowingly and gave the order for Ed and me to take our places on the ice. On the command to go the three of us shoved off. The sail billowed again and we jumped on.

"This part will be a little slower at first," Tommy said to Isobel as we cruised north to run along the shoreline.

"That's understandable given the wind," she said. "Still, we're doing just under fifteen knots."

Tommy gave her a funny look. "What makes you think so?"

"I timed how long it takes us to pass those two red buoys that run along the south shore of the harbour. If I remember my charts correctly, they're exactly one mile apart, and it took us just under four minutes to pass from one to the other."

From Tommy's expression I could see he didn't feel quite so superior now. Isobel was full of surprises.

We passed through the Western Gap and continued west. To the left was open water. Lake Ontario was too huge to freeze over completely during winter. Where the water was shallower, ice formed in a hundred-yard-wide shelf along the north shore, but without the protection of the islands the ice became really bumpy. Mostly ice floes jammed together by the wind, it was rough enough for those of us standing, but we could bend our knees and let our legs act like shock absorbers on a wagon. Poor Isobel, though, was being bounced an awful lot as she tried to keep her seat in the cockpit. Tommy let her bump up and down for about thirty seconds before he asked, "Maybe it's a little too rough for m'lady?"

"Yes," Isobel admitted. There was a reserved tone in her voice, though, as if she had just made up her mind about something.

Tommy swung hard around, and we headed back through the gap's level ice. Leisurely, we tacked down to the Eastern Gap so we could get a good, fast run. As soon as Tommy had a long, smooth stretch in front of us, he said, "Okay, m'lady, get out the watch and tell us how fast we're going on this trip."

Happily, Isobel took out her watch again as the *Marinion* began accelerating. "Thirty miles an hour!" she called out. "Forty miles an hour!" she said thirty seconds later. "Fifty!" she shouted excitedly at the one-minute mark.

At this speed the port runner started to hike. Normally, with a paying passenger onboard, Tommy would have backed off on the sail, but he had some dignity to recover. He gestured for me move out to counterbalance the wind. I had never stood on the beam at this speed before, and common sense would normally have kicked in or at least told me I should be frightened. Having Isobel onboard changed that. No wonder there was a superstition about women on ships being bad luck. It wasn't the woman's fault, of course. It was guys doing stupid things trying to impress them. I knew for sure that Tommy was showing off a little.

The only person not frightened was Isobel. She looked as if she were in a room full of people wishing her a happy birthday. Her expression didn't change even as we skidded over two-inch-high cracks in the ice or hit patches of washboard that made our boat shudder and roar.

I felt jealous as Isobel glanced back at Tommy in admiration. With the tiller in his hand he reminded me of one of the fearless Viking explorers in my father's books.

When my runner began to lift again, I gratefully leaned back, knowing this would return Isobel's attention to me. Ed crossed over to join me.

"That's it, Ed, Simcoe!" Tommy shouted. "All the way out. Let's see what this old girl can do."

I did as I was told, holding tight to the shroud line and leaning backward until my outstretched body was as far out as my arms would allow. The ice was whirring a few feet below me at nearly sixty miles an hour. For the first few seconds I was nearly paralyzed with fear. After that I was still terrified, but the thought of Isobel watching me made me bolder. I tilted my head and felt the frigid wind rush over my face while I gazed straight up at the patches straining on our old yellow sail, which billowed out like a crazy quilt on a clothesline against the clear blue sky.

"Hey, where are you going?" I heard Tommy bark. "Don't!"

I looked up, thinking I must have been doing something wrong again, but for once it wasn't me. Isobel was standing at the front end of the cockpit. Tommy couldn't drop the sail without hitting her, so all he could do was shout while holding the tiller bar and sheet. Isobel seemed to know this. Instead of obeying Tommy, she calmly stepped out of the cockpit and walked up the centre timber, the thin wooden beam that connected to the runner beams and masts. "No! Sit, blast it!" Tommy screamed.

I was too far out on the runner to do anything. Ed started moving forward, but Isobel spotted him coming and paused just short of his reach.

*Whack!*

"Holy —" Tommy almost cussed, but he caught himself.

We had all been so busy watching Isobel that we had failed to notice a big pressure crack coming straight at us. With a crash the boat lifted three feet off the ice. We flew for at least fifty feet before the *Marinion* landed with a loud *thwack* on the ice. Both Ed and I lost our footing on the runner beam, but we managed to hang on to the shroud lines. Astern, Tommy stopped himself from being thrown out of the cockpit. He actually bent the iron tiller bar pulling himself back in without flipping the *Marinion*.

As soon as we all recovered, we looked around but saw no Isobel.

"Oh, dear Lord! She must have fallen off!" Tommy yelled, heeling hard to port while we scanned behind us.

No Isobel. Nothing but bare, empty ice for a thousand yards.

"Do you think she fell through a hole in the ice?" Ed asked.

Tommy's face went white at the suggestion. He slackened the sheet so we could have a better look at the pressure crack we had just jumped. All three of us expected to see her body crumpled on the far side of it.

"Oh, please don't slow down!" a voice from above said.

We glanced up, and there was Isobel, perched in the starboard ratlines at the top of the mast.

"Hey ... what ...?" Tommy sputtered. "Come down off there!" he finally spat out.

"Why? The view is splendid. I can see the spire of St. James' Cathedral from here. That's at least two miles away."

Ed smirked at Tommy. "She's right. The view is splendid."

Down below, we were all getting an eyeful of windswept petticoats, dainty black boots, silk stockings, and lacy knee garters. But for the moment the view seemed lost on Tommy.

"I don't care!" he bellowed. "That spot's off-limits to passengers. It's for crew members only!"

"Oh," Isobel said thoughtfully, "then may I please be a crew member?"

*"Whaaaaat!"* Tommy screeched. I was sure they had heard him all the way over at St. James' Cathedral.

"I wish very much to be a crew member," she announced. "May I? Please?"

"No!" Tommy snapped. "You can't be a crew member!"

"Why not?"

"Because you know nothing about sailing."

"Nonsense. I've been racing sailboats since I was a child. I've even raced in Nantucket."

"What? Nan-fwhat it?"

"Nantucket," I said. "It's a place on the ocean."

"Precisely," Isobel said. "So can I be part of your crew?"

"No!" Tommy roared.

"My father and I have competed in races around the world. But this is ever so much more thrilling."

Tommy brought the boat to a dead halt. "I don't care if you've sailed all the way to Tokyo, China, lady!"

Under normal circumstances I would have pointed out to Tommy that Tokyo was in Japan, not China, but something told me this wouldn't be a good time to do that. Veins were bulging on either side of his forehead, and without even thinking about it, he had bent the iron tiller bar back to its original shape.

"Come down off there!" he ordered Isobel.

"No," she said calmly.

*"No?"* Tommy exploded.

"I paid for a one-hour excursion, and by my watch I still have forty-five minutes left. Take me to the Eastern Gap, please."

"I'm going to take you right back to the shore and throw you off my boat."

"Very well, but I'm not coming down. Everyone in the harbour will see me up here and wonder how I came to be stranded on your topmast."

"Because you climbed up there."

"To escape your foul temper. It really is most dreadful, you know."

*"It is not!"*

"Oh, look," Isobel said primly, "I do believe the Harbour Police boat is coming our way."

Sure enough, the bull boat was turning toward us at its usual ponderous pace. Whenever a vessel stopped for no apparent reason in the middle of the bay, the bulls came out to see if anything was wrong.

"Okay," Tommy said. "You win. Come down and you can be a member of the crew."

"No."

"What! I said you won. Just come down."

"I don't believe you."

"Are you calling me a liar, you spoiled little ... brat?"

"If I came down now, you'd just put me ashore and never let me sail again."

The glare of aggravation on Tommy's face confirmed everything Isobel had said. The police boat was now a few hundred yards away and still closing.

"Okay," Tommy finally said. "What do I have to do?"

"Raise the sail and let's finish my hour."

"Sure."

"And when we return to York Street, you'll tell all the other boat skippers that I'm now officially part of your crew."

"No!" Tommy hollered.

"Suit yourself," Isobel said, sighing. "But it would

be a real cause for concern if I were to fall out of the rigging just as that police boat arrived."

Isobel lifted one foot off the ratlines and kicked it in the air. "Oh!" she cried. "Oh, dear! I think my feet are slipping."

"Not a chance," Tommy growled.

Isobel raised her other foot off the shrouds and kicked both feet out as if she were swimming in midair. The bull boat was now a hundred yards away.

"It's getting frightfully dangerous up here!" Isobel wailed in a mock-pathetic voice. "And, oh, I believe my left hand is about to let go! Oh!" She released the shroud and actually had the strength to hang by one hand from the topmast until Tommy caved in at last.

"Okay, okay!" he said. "Get your feet back on those rungs."

Isobel easily swung back onto the ratlines like a trapeze artist. "Very good. You may sail when ready, Captain."

Tommy shook his head angrily, then nodded at Ed and me. For the third time this trip we pushed off. Tommy slowly raised the sail. Then, gently, the boat began to move again.

"Faster!" Isobel commanded.

Muttering under his breath, Tommy adjusted the sheet and we started accelerating.

The Harbour Police boat swung alongside. "Is everything all right?" a wind-burnt police sergeant shouted at us through a megaphone.

"Couldn't be better!" Tommy yelled back.

Ed and I nodded, and Isobel waved gaily from the top rigging.

The sergeant frowned when he saw Isobel but said nothing. There was no law against climbing ratlines.

"Can't we go faster?" Isobel asked Tommy as we pulled away from the police.

"Faster?"

"Yes, I recently read that an iceboat on the Hudson River reached a speed of one hundred and forty-four miles per hour. We haven't gone even half as fast as that."

Tommy looked as if he had just been called a farmer. "Okay, m'lady. You asked for it."

Tommy, Ed, and I reefed the *Marinion* for maximum speed. We again sailed to the Eastern Gap and hauled around to position ourselves for the best advantage to the wind. It was a better-than-average day with a strong, steady breeze and lots of flat, open ice. Tommy let out the sail, and we took off.

"Twenty miles per hour!" Isobel called from above. She had that stupid watch out again.

The *Marinion* continued to accelerate.

"Thirty-five miles per hour!" she cried.

A pair of pigeons flew in and kept abreast of us for a few minutes, but we slowly left them behind.

"Forty-five miles per hour!" Isobel announced.

Tommy ignored her.

"Fifty-five miles per hour!"

Tommy still ignored her.

"Sixty!" she said ten seconds later.

A mile a minute. That was the fastest I'd ever gone.

"Sixty-five! No, seventy!"

Now even Ed and Tommy seemed impressed.

"Simcoe, get over with Ed on the port runner beam!" Tommy ordered.

As soon as I reached Ed, Isobel called out, "Pressure crack dead ahead. Steer to starboard."

"Hey, I'm skipper of this boat!" Tommy snapped. "Not you!"

*Bang!* We hit the pressure crack. It was just a little one, but at high speed we got quite a jolt. Ed and I glanced at Tommy, who was biting his lip.

"Okay, so she saw a pressure crack," he growled.

"Deadhead two hundred yards ahead," Isobel warned. "Looks like a beer barrel. Washboard on the port tack."

That meant we should steer to starboard, but I think Isobel was trying to be diplomatic. Instead of giving a command, she was letting Tommy decide the obvious. It was a question of whether he was willing to take a hint or not.

Tommy waited until the very last second, then yelled, "Hang on, boys!" He swung the tiller hard to starboard.

The *Marinion*'s runners bit into the ice. As we changed direction, I felt as if I weighed three hundred pounds when we leaned into the turn.

"Gee, Tom!" Ed groaned through gritted teeth.

We were both standing at forty-five-degree angles. I looked up and saw Isobel doing the same thing in the shrouds.

Ed peered up, too. "That's not a girl. That's a chimpanzee."

*"Whoooooooeeeeee!"* the chimp called out to no one in particular.

Even Tommy smiled when he saw how much Isobel

was enjoying the ride. Admiration crossed his face and then he remembered he was supposed to be mad at her. That lasted for about fifteen more minutes. Eventually, he got over his anger and started joking again. Tommy had a hard time staying mad at anyone, especially when he was sailing. We reached the Western Gap again and slowed down for the return trip.

"Is your hour up yet?" Tommy finally asked.

"Officially, yes," Isobel said. "Ten minutes ago. But you had to make good for that stopover in the middle of the bay. I'm not paying you to sit still."

I expected a tart comment from Tommy, but he had a strange expression on his face. I had seen the same look on a male dog's face after it came back from a few days at the vet.

We returned to the docking area. Because of the low speed limit for all iceboats as they approached the docking area, Tommy was forced to bring the *Marinion* in slow and steady. Even from two hundred yards away, people noticed Isobel up top and began pointing. The same game of hockey we had stopped on the way out again came to a halt.

Isobel waved to a well-dressed couple passing on the starboard side in an open electric car. "Hello, Mr and Mrs. Eaton!"

Mrs. Eaton's mouth gaped wide enough to catch a lake perch. Mr. Eaton almost ran over a chestnut vendor.

"Well, I never!" another woman squawked as she strolled arm in arm with an officer from the 48th Highlanders of Canada along the ice promenade.

"It must be cold up there," we heard the officer say to his companion.

"It must be cold down there," Isobel said, referring to the army man's kilt.

Even Tommy couldn't help laughing at that one. The couple turned their heads and rushed away.

"Ma, I want to go up, too!" a small boy said to his mother as we passed by. He began crying when his mother said no.

The anchorage was dead ahead. Tommy expertly steered to an open parking space between the *Digger* and the *Kipper* and dropped the sail. As part of our shutdown routine, Ed and I tied down the sail so it wouldn't catch the wind by accident, and Tommy removed the tiller bar and turned the stern runner upside down so the *Marinion* would stay put.

Isobel remained motionless in the rigging.

"Hey, you can come down, now!" Tommy called out.

"I'm waiting," Isobel said quietly.

"For what?"

"You know darn well what. You promised."

*Here we go again*, I thought.

"Hey, Tommy, what's that caught in your rigging?" Fred Phelan yelled from the firepit. "A seagull?"

The other skippers and crewmen turned and looked. "Too big for a seagull," someone else said. "Maybe it's an albatross."

Everyone except Tommy laughed. "More like a vulture," he grumbled under his breath.

"My name is Isobel!" she shouted to the sailors by the campfire. "I'm the newest member of the

*Marinion*'s crew."

A chorus of hoots, whistles, and catcalls made Tommy speak up in Isobel's defence. "She climbs those ratlines better than anyone else I've seen, and she has more sailing time in than most of you combined. Last summer she even sailed to Nan's Bucket."

"Where's that?" asked Billy Fisher, skipper of the *Temeraire*.

Tommy's face was a complete blank. "In the States, of course."

"Well, come on down, little missy, and have something warm by the fire," Hector McDonell, Tommy's father, invited. His eyes nearly fell out of his head as Isobel slid down the rigging without using the rungs. "Would the young lady like some tea?" Hector asked as Isobel came closer.

Tommy was already shaking his head.

But Isobel said, "Yes, I would be delighted," before he could get any words out.

The crowd of thirty-odd men fell over themselves stepping backward to allow Isobel to approach the fire directly. Women were a rare sight in this area. Female sailors were unheard of. A seat improvised out of a butter crate thoughtfully padded with a horsehair blanket appeared out of nowhere. Tea in a clean china mug was quickly produced. As Isobel gracefully pulled off her fur-trimmed leather gloves, silence fell over the gathering. She noticed my eyes straying to one glove. It had a split leather patch clumsily sewn into the palm. The patch was meant to give her a better grip on the ropes; she had planned her stunt all along. Isobel flashed a tiny smile at me, and we both knew I wasn't going to say a thing to Ed or Tommy.

"Thank you," she said, accepting the chipped old tea mug from Hector with both hands.

"Where did you learn to sail?" Fred Phelan asked.

"I was born on a *goélette*," Isobel said. "Off Corsica."

"Where's that?" Tommy whispered to me.

"Same place Napoleon was born," I told him.

"Well, that figures," Ed snickered, giving Tommy a nudge in the ribs.

"What's a *goélette*?" I asked.

"A French schooner," Hector said.

Without a shred of self-consciousness, Isobel began talking sailboating to some of the oldest and most experienced mariners in our group.

"When I first came to this city, I was particularly intrigued," she said, "to note that most Toronto iceboats are equipped as a lateen rig while the boats in Kingston, New York, are Bermuda-rigged with a jib and mainsail. It gives your boats a very attractive Mediterranean look, but doesn't that reduce the sail area?"

"Well, we likes the lateen sail because it's more weatherly," said old Mr. Parkinson, skipper of the *Snow Flake*. "With our lateens we can sail closer to the wind because the yard cuts cleaner. We gets more wind out of less sail, and we don't need the extra rigging and gear a jib and mainsail need."

I had no idea what Old Parky was saying, but Isobel nodded as if the geezer were spouting perfect English.

"I noticed that your boats are heavier here, too," she continued. "Some even have steel spars and deck stays while the ones on the Hudson River are much lighter."

Old Parky grinned. "Well, ice conditions are much rougher here than in Kingston. No doubt if we took our boats to New York, they'd beat us clean because they're lighter, but if a Kingston boat came here, it'd likely be smashed to toothypicks before it cleared Hanlan's Point."

"Them tatties ready?" Skipper McQuire asked his sheet tender.

"Looks so."

"Well, dig in, boys."

Everyone reached in and grabbed a blackened spud with their bare hands. I picked one up, but even with leather mitts on I had to toss it back and forth to keep from screaming in pain.

"Would the miss like a potato?" Hector asked.

"Why ... yes ... but ..." Isobel made a face as if she were afraid to make a fool of herself the way I had.

Hector smiled and took out his belt knife. Snapping open the blade, he stabbed a potato and presented the knife handle to Isobel. "Just let that cool off a bit, miss."

"'Ere, and let's put a sprinkle of salt and pepper on there for you," Eddie Durnan offered.

For another twenty minutes Isobel exchanged questions and comments with the older men, while the younger ones looked on, too shy to speak up. "She knows her boats," Skipper Fischer of the *Silver Heels* commented. Isobel was explaining that she had only been living in Toronto for four months because her parents travelled a lot. Her mother was French. Her father was an American who worked for a British company that invested in promising companies around the British Empire.

"I've lived in more than twenty cities so far, and I fear my moving days aren't over yet," she said.

You could almost hear two dozen hearts breaking at once. Suddenly, Isobel's face froze in horror. If hanging from a topmast at sixty miles per hour didn't make her blink, I wondered what hideous vision could so frighten her now.

I followed her gaze and saw someone approaching. It was the woman I had mistaken for a suit of armour beside Isobel on Christmas Eve. I was now close enough to see that she was only a few years older than Isobel, but she still resembled a walking suit of armour and she definitely wasn't happy. Her lips were drawn wide in a grimace, and steam blasted out of both nostrils. There was nowhere to run, so Isobel tried to play innocent. "Fräulein von Tirpitz! There you are!"

"Izobel! Izobel!" the apparition sputtered. "Where have you been? I have been looking all over for you! You were zupposed to stay rrright behind me in the market."

"I lost you in the cheeses, Fräulein."

"I have spent the past two hours walking through this filthy place searching for you, and no less a person than Mrs. Eaton informs me you chust zay 'Hello' to them from the top of one of these ... these ..."

"Iceboats," I volunteered.

"Hooligan contrrraptionz!" the woman hissed. "And now I find you here zurrounded by these ..."

"Iceboaters," I suggested.

"Roughianz, und eating ..."

"A potato with pepper?"

"A potato with pepper?" the woman shrieked.

"Pepper! Izobel, you know very well you are not allowed to eat pepper!"

"She isn't?" several skippers said in unison. "Why not?"

Fräulein von Tirpitz looked as if she would rather spit than speak to us.

"Because Dr. Kellogg says spices are bad for girls," Isobel said wearily.

"Dr. Kellogg?" one of the skippers questioned.

"The cereal guy," I said.

"Does Dr. Kellogg have daughters of his own?" Hector asked.

"No," Isobel's keeper said. "But he is a doctor and knows these things better than a bunch of ... of ..."

"Rrriff-rrraff," I said.

"Iceboaterz," Fräulein von Tirpitz said as if that were even worse. "Dr. Kellogg zays that young ladiez must avoid zpices of any kind because it excites their passions. Now, Izobel, come!"

Sadly, Isobel stood and trudged past us to join the Fräulein.

"Is that what happened to you?" Tommy asked. "Too much pepper?"

Isobel turned and stuck out her tongue at Tommy. She still had the potato in her hand.

"And what is that you are holding?" von Tirpitz shrieked. "*Mein Gott!* Is that a knife?"

"Oh, that's mine," Hector said, stepping forward to retrieve his knife.

"You giff a knife to a young lady?"

"To eat a potato."

"With pepper! I think I shall make a reportz to the police."

"Fräulein von Tirpitz," Isobel interjected. "We're going to be late for my French and piano lessons."

For once I was glad to see that stupid watch in her hand.

Fräulein von Tirpitz took out her own watch and compared it to Isobel's. "Ach! Zo. Then we must leave immediately. Come!" The Fräulein gave it hard starboard rudder and began steaming away. When Isobel didn't fall into step, she shouted, "Come! *Schnell!*"

Isobel gave us a quick wave and fell into line behind von Tirpitz's wake.

"That's the last we'll see of her," Ed said with a sigh.

"I don't think so," Hector said as he cleaned off the knife on his sleeve.

"Well, she's the best climber on the crew," I said.

"A woman crew member," Tommy muttered. "Cripes, we'll be signing on Chinamen next."

"Oh," I murmured.

"Oh?"

"I was going to ask you about that."

7

# Anchors Hwei

## January 19, 1907

His name was Hwei Coon. His uncle owned the Chinese laundry next to our house. Although we had lived beside each other for more than a year, I had never actually said a word to Hwei, even though I frequently saw him staggering down the street under huge bundles of freshly starched bed linen or coaxing weird-looking vegetables to grow in his uncle's postage stamp backyard garden. I didn't even know if he spoke English. Still, we always nodded at each other as we passed on the street.

Then, on the first day of school after the New Year break, our principal, Walter Rogers, entered my class as we were about to sing "God Save the King." We fell silent. Mr. Rogers's nickname was Wailing Walt because of the two-foot-long leather strap that hung from a nail at the corner of his desk. It had a notch at the end that was said to leave a welt on your hands that lasted for weeks.

Mr. Rogers glanced at the doorway and waved his hand. In walked Hwei like a sheep being coaxed into a wolf pen. Our teacher, Miss Worthington, lowered the pitch pipe from her lips. "And is this our new student, Mr. Rogers?"

"It is, indeed, Miss Worthington. Boys and girls, this is Hwei Coon, and he's now a student here at Parkdale Public School."

*"Coon!"* snorted Jack MacGregor in the back. Nearly the whole class exploded in laughter. Hwei's face turned red.

"MacGregor. My office," Mr. Rogers said in a low voice. In an instant the class was quiet. MacGregor's chair made a shrill, scraping sound on the wooden floor, and he shuffled out of the room like a condemned man. "I know you'll all be kind and considerate to Hwei," Mr. Rogers said, a bit of menace in his words. "I want him treated exactly like anyone else in this room. Am I understood?"

There was a long, nervous silence.

"Am I understood?"

"Yes, sir!" the whole class chorused.

"Good. We understand each other then. I'll leave you to your studies. Thank you, Miss Worthington."

"Thank you, Mr. Rogers."

The principal exited, and we all exhaled together, including Miss Worthington.

"Hwei, would you take that seat there?"

"Yes, Miss Worthington," Hwei said with just a trace of an accent.

"Oh, good. You do know English," Miss Worthington said with relief.

"I can speak English, but I cannot write it, ma'am."

"I speakee but no writee," Tim Matthews said in a mock-Chinese accent, and the class erupted in laughter again. He always said dumb things like that.

"Matthews! In my office now!" Mr. Rogers boomed from just outside the door.

Matthews looked as if he had been struck by lightning out of a clear sky. "But ... but ...?" he sputtered, glancing at Miss Worthington for rescue.

"Now!" Mr. Rogers ordered.

"You'd better go, Tim," Miss Worthington said. "Don't make it worse for yourself."

Slowly, Tim stood and shuffled out, leaning backward as if an invisible hand were forcing him out the door. Next we heard three sets of feet walk heavily along the wooden hall floor toward the principal's office. Then a door squeaked opened and closed with a loud bang that made us all jump in our seats. After that the class sat in agonized silence.

Miss Worthington seemed as paralyzed as the rest of us. Suddenly, she remembered the anthem. "Oh, yes!" she said, picking up the pitch pipe. She blew a long, reedy C. The class hummed the note in response, and with Miss Worthington conducting, we began to sing.

"God save *thwack!* our *graaaaaacious thwack!* king. Long ... live *ourrrr thwack!* Noble king. *Thwack!* God *thwack!* save *thwack!* our ... *thwack!* king ... *thwack! Thwack! Thwack!*"

It definitely wasn't the king who needed saving that morning. We finished our anthem, Miss Worthington led us in the Lord's Prayer, and then Jack and Tim re-entered the room red-faced. Tim had already been crying, and Jack was obviously trying to hold back tears. They were prize jerks, but as much as I disliked the two, I still felt sorry for them.

Hwei stared down at his desk. It was Tim's own big mouth that had gotten him into trouble, but Hwei had correctly guessed he would receive the blame.

All through the morning Tim whispered threats and insults at Hwei. I was just one desk to Hwei's right, so I knew he heard them. When the recess bell rang, while the rest of the class shrugged into their winter coats, Hwei remained at his desk.

"You can go outside now," Miss Worthington said.

"I think I would rather stay here," Hwei told her.

"School regulations, Hwei," Miss Worthington said. "You must go outside. Fresh air is good for you."

Already outside were the shrieks of kids enjoying their release, however temporary, from the boredom of school.

Miss Worthington smiled encouragingly. "See? They're having fun out there. Fresh air never hurt anyone."

A lot she knew.

Because we were neighbours, I felt sort of obligated to wait for Hwei as he reluctantly put on his jacket and picked up his mitts and hat. "C'mon, I'll show you a good place to hide," I offered. I'd had my run-ins with Tim and Jack, as well. With Miss Worthington shooing us out the door, we stepped outside.

But there was no hiding today. Every kid from every class was standing at the door waiting to gawk at the first Chinese student ever to attend our school. The promise of watching him likely take a beating from Tim was icing on the cake.

*"Chinky-chinky-chinaman!"* a little first-grader yelled at Hwei. Then he ran screaming into a group of older kids for protection.

Behind Hwei's back a pair of students began pulling the sides of their eyes out and bowing back and forth to each other and making stupid sounds that they thought sounded like Chinese.

"Manley! Van Allen! Newton! In my office now!" Mr. Rogers thundered from inside the school. He didn't even open a window. The entire school yard of kids froze as three more boys trudged unhappily into the school. Tim, very menacing a few seconds ago, now wilted like a dandelion. He turned and ran as far as he could get from Hwei.

It was a very quiet recess after that. Kids stood in silent clusters around the school yard. They were afraid even to look at Hwei as the two of us hunched in the shelter of the south wall of the school stamping our feet and flapping our arms, trying to keep warm until recess was over.

"So where did you go to school before?" I asked Hwei.

"I didn't."

"What? Every kid has to go to school."

"Not if you are Chinese. My uncle had to ask permission seven times before they finally agreed to let me in. It was not easy. Chinese people are not allowed to vote, so we had a hard time finding a politician even willing to talk to us."

"Why?"

Hwei glanced at me as if I were either blind or stupid. He tapped his chest. "Because I am Chinese. My uncle taught me how to read and write as best he could, but my parents want me to get a proper education with a certificate."

"Your parents? Are they here, too?"

"No, they are still in China."

"Don't you miss them?"

"At first, very much. I also miss my boat."

"What boat?"

"We lived on a boat in China. I did not step on dry land until I was nearly three."

"You're joking."

"No. My father made his living moving goods back and forth in his boat. During the day, we sailed. At night we put down anchor and slept. We ate on the boat and slept on the boat."

"What about school?"

Hwei shrugged. "No school. It was fun."

"Why did you leave?"

"Small boat. Big family. My parents have seven sons. Too big for one boat. When my uncle came to Canada, he had no one to help him with laundry, so he asked his big brother, my father, for a son."

"Why didn't he just get married and have his own children?"

"The Canadian government charges Chinese people five hundred dollars each just to come to Canada. Few Chinese men can afford to bring their wives to Canada."

"Why?" I asked. Five hundred dollars was the price of a house. That didn't sound right to me.

Hwei gave me that irritated look again and sighed. "Because Canadians are afraid Canada will turn Chinese if too many of us are allowed to come here." He laughed without smiling. "The banks will not give Chinese people a loan to pay the government tax, and it would take my father years to raise that kind of money on his own."

"So your uncle paid five hundred dollars just to let you come here?"

"Yes. In return I work for nothing."

"Why do Chinese people want to come here so much?"

"The same reason most people want to come to Canada. Things are hard back home. In China, Canada is called Golden Mountain because it is believed you can make a lot of money if you are willing to work hard. Many Chinese men come here to make money to send home. I am working for my uncle for free, but when I grow up, my uncle will give me the laundry and he will go home with a fortune to retire. Then I will send for a son from China."

"Do you miss China?"

"I miss my family. I miss sailing my boat."

"Would you like to try ice sailing?"

"Ice sailing?"

"Yes. Sailboats that go over the ice."

"That is not possible. You are teasing me."

"No. I do it every weekend. Our skipper's looking for experienced crew. I'll ask him."

A loud metallic clatter exploded over our heads.

"There's the bell," I said. "Time to go back in."

A few days later my father found an article about Hwei in the *Toronto Daily Star*. Under the title PUBLIC SCHOOL ADMITS FIRST CHINESE STUDENT, the article described how Principal Rogers was forced to give nearly ten students the strap for calling Hwei names in the first week. The newspaper quoted Principal Rogers, who said: "No doubt the little Chinaman will make good progress."

The next Saturday I took Hwei out to see the iceboat fleet. Tommy and Ed were already there. To our surprise and concealed delight, Isobel came skipping down the shore bank while a sullen Fräulein von Tirpitz glared from the back of a chauffer-driven car. Isobel had somehow convinced her parents to let her learn how to ice-sail because the sport was so popular with the millionaires in New York State. Today she was much more appropriately dressed in a young woman's bicycle skirt, which was like a very baggy pair of pants.

Some of the men hooted at the sight of Isobel, but when they caught sight of Hwei, they fell silent in amazement.

"Who's that?" someone asked.

"He's trying out for crew on the *Marinion*," I said.

"Hey, Tommy," a loudmouth skipper called Downtown Brown said with a smirk, "looks like you do have a Chinaman's chance of winning the Durnan Cup."

Everyone exploded in laugher except for the *Marinion*'s crew. Hwei grinned politely, but I could tell from his eyes that he didn't like the joke.

"Well, let's find out if he can sail," Tommy said, wanting to get out of there quickly.

"While you're heading out, how about a quick race, Tommy?" Downtown challenged. He owned a small homemade boat named the *Ice Pick*. His crew consisted of two burly longshoremen who, when sober, knew their stuff.

Tommy studied Downtown and his boys. Downtown looked fine, but the other two had probably just rolled down from the Walker House Hotel on Front and York Streets. They seemed steady on their feet, but judging by the way they were perspiring in ten-below-zero weather, they had spent most of their week's wages last night on beer and were still feeling the effects.

Shrugging, Tommy said, "If you want." Obviously, with three new crew members, the last thing he wanted was a race, but Tommy wouldn't back down to a bunch of mutts like the guys on the *Ice Pick*.

"We've got six bits that says we can beat you to the West Entrance and back," Downtown said.

The *Ice Pick* was as good a boat as the *Marinion*. With today's conditions — cold, crisp, with an eastbound wind blowing at five knots over smooth ice — both vessels would fly fast if trimmed right.

Six bits meant seventy-five cents. That was a lot of money to bet on a boat boasting a half-trained crew plus a new man who had never seen an iceboat let alone race one. No one there would have blamed Tommy for bowing out, but he never backed down from anything.

"Make it a buck even," Tommy said, and he and Downtown shook on it. "Just give us five minutes to show our new man the ropes."

Downtown bowed. "Most honourable pleasure," he purred, and his crew guffawed.

"What an oaf," Isobel muttered as we followed Tommy to the *Marinion*. Hwei said something else in Chinese, which was probably more or less the same thing.

When shown the *Marinion*, Hwei took one look at the tall, spindly contraption and laughed. "This boat cannot sail."

"Oh, she'll sail all right," Tommy said. "The question is — can you hang on?"

"I think I can," Hwei said, showing Tommy two young hands already rock-hard with calluses.

Ed grinned. "A working man's hands. Now that's more like it!" He winked at Isobel and me. "No offence to your Lordship and Lady."

Tommy showed Hwei the basic ropes and rigging of the boat and how far the boom swung as we changed tack. "Now the difference between this boat and the one you're used to will be the speed. These things move faster than anything else in the world."

Hwei nodded, but I knew he thought Tommy was teasing him. Why not? That was what all white people seemed to do to him. Still, Hwei seemed game to try.

"Got it?" Tommy asked.

"Got it!" Hwei said eagerly.

"Okay, just follow Ed and Bertie's lead. Isobel, after we're underway, you go to the top and give us ice reports."

For once Isobel didn't argue with Tommy. Ed told Isobel to stand with him on the starboard, while Hwei and I took up position behind the port runner. I explained that when the race began the four of us would push from the front while Tommy shoved from the stern. Hwei nodded.

"*Marinion* ready!" Tommy called out, and in a few seconds Downtown Brown and his boys swaggered out to their boat. Well, sort of swaggered-staggered.

Tommy glanced at Isobel, Hwei, and I standing like three sheep by the front runners. "This ... is going to be an interesting race," he said, and he and Ed chuckled.

Informal iceboat races happened all the time. To keep one boat from scooping the other's wind, the craft lined up fifty feet apart, using York Street as a starting mark. It was agreed that each boat would round the marker at the Western Gap and then race back to the finish at York. As senior skipper on site, Fred Phelan was asked to start us off with the count.

"Ready!" Phelan hollered, and we all crouched at our places. "Set!" he yelled.

Beside me I could feel Hwei's muscles hunching like a tiger's.

"Go!"

With five of us pushing, the *Marinion* left the starting line easily. In less than ten strides we were up to full running speed. With three sailors, two of them drunk, the *Ice Pick* made a much less impressive beginning.

"Boarding ... now!" Tommy shouted and, for a first-time try, we all managed to climb up pretty well. At this point Ed usually hauled up the sail himself while Tommy kept the tiller bar straight. To our surprise, both Hwei and Isobel were by his side in an instant, and together they raised the sail, alternating hands like two veterans.

*Kawhumpthk!* cracked the old sail as the steady breeze filled it. The boom snapped to port, and Hwei knew enough to duck. Isobel was already moving forward to take her place in the rigging.

"Monkey girl," Hwei said to me, watching her effortlessly scramble up the improved ratlines Tommy had put up for her.

Despite its rough launch, the *Ice Pick* was also picking up speed, and soon we were scudding along bow-to-bow toward the Western Gap.

"Pretty fast," Hwei admitted.

"You ain't seen nothing yet," I said, regretting that the wind was fairly weak today.

"Twelve knots!" Isobel called out.

The *Ice Pick* was starting to pull ahead of us, partly because it only had three people onboard and partly because some idiot on a motorized bicycle suddenly wobbled out in front of the *Marinion*, causing Tommy to lose valuable seconds to avoid hitting the fool.

The crew of the *Ice Pick* looked back and laughed at us until they hit a pressure crack that sent their craft flying two feet into the air. When it landed twenty feet later, the impact caused the two red-faced crew members to lose their footing and half fall off. Their feet dragged on the ice while they hung on for dear life with their hands, allowing us to catch up again. As they clambered aboard, Downtown Brown gave them a blast of profanity for their clumsiness.

"Hey, watch the language!" Ed shouted. "We have a lady in our midst."

Isobel fired back a barrage of profanity at the *Ice Pick* that almost made Tommy fall off the stern.

The *Ice Pick* was closest to the tree marker at the turn, and we slipped back a boat length because we were forced to swing wide to avoid hitting our opponent. Now, heading against the wind, it was a tacking battle for both boats. The morning sunlight in our eyes made it difficult to see the ice clearly, but Isobel was able to warn Tommy about ridges or slushy spots from her vantage point in the rigging. So we began to move ahead as the *Ice Pick* blundered into a couple of slush ponds.

With each change of tack, Ed, Hwei, and I had to swap sides of the boat while ducking under the swinging boom. Hwei caught on fast as we showed him how to lean out to counterbalance against the wind and then crouch and dive under the boom as Tommy ordered another change of tack.

"Soft ice one hundred yards, clear starboard!" Isobel called out.

"Steering starboard!" Tommy shouted, and we swung hard to starboard.

Downtown was a boor, but no dummy. After wallowing through a couple of patches of soft ice, he figured out why Tommy was missing them. Downtown could hear Isobel's updates to Tommy, and he began to change tack every time she shouted to us.

Tack by tack, Downtown and his boat started to pull ahead, mostly because he was able to use Isobel's warnings against us. Downtown's crew was definitely slower on the tack changes, but his men made it up in speed once the sail was set. Just before we pulled up to the halfway marker, Isobel cried, "Pressure ridge starboard!"

Immediately, both boats swung to port. "Thanks, missy!" Brown hollered. "Just keep those ice reports coming!"

"Reverse tack quick!" Isobel commanded while Ed, Hwei, and I were still halfway to our starboard stations.

"Port!" Tommy yelled, reversing the boom and tiller while Ed, Hwei, and I hung on against the momentum of the unexpected turn.

The *Marinion* turned, and out of the morning glare a big patch of deep slush loomed in front of us, then passed on the starboard side as we turned. Slow on their feet, Downtown's crewmen couldn't reverse fast enough, and they ploughed into the slush with a heavy *pltttttttthhhhhhhhhhhhh*. The next sound we heard was swearing as the two crewmen pitched face down and took an ice-water bath in the soggy mess.

"Nice," Ed said. "She deked Downtown into the slush."

"Ice report. Slush ahead!" Isobel barked at Downtown and his crew as we left them behind. She then let loose with a cackle that sent chills up our spines.

"There's something scary about that lady," Tommy said under his breath.

The *Ice Pick* was out of the race, so the bay was all ours as we ran for home.

"You did great, Hwei," Tommy said as we lowered the sail and the boat glided to rest among the other craft. "What do you think of iceboat racing?"

"You are all crazy."

"We like crazy," Ed said.

Hwei smiled. "Good. Me, too."

When the *Ice Pick* limped in five minutes later, Tommy said to Downtown, "It seems you didn't even have a Chinaman's chance."

Sourly, Downtown and his crew paid up. No beer for them tonight.

"One dollar split five ways isn't the Irish Sweepstakes," Ed said.

Tommy shrugged. "It'll buy a cone of chips on the way home."

Even though she obviously didn't need the money, Isobel gratefully accepted her four nickels as if they were gold guineas. For us the money meant food; for Isobel it was proof she was a sailor.

We went back out for another two hours of sailing and then decided to call it a day because the ice was turning mushy.

"Oh, and this is for you," Isobel said, handing Tommy a dollar as we anchored at York Street.

"What's this?" he asked.

"For the iceboat lesson. I told my father you charged a dollar a session. He wouldn't have agreed to my being here unless I insisted you were a professional."

"A whole dollar?" Tommy said, incredulous.

"Don't be so impressed," she said as she ran up the bank to her car. "My dancing instructor charges two."

Hwei and I walked home to Defoe Street. We resisted the urge to spend our twenty cents each on candy or chips. Our families both needed the money.

As we approached the laundry, Hwei said, "Bertie, can I ask a favour?"

"Sure."

"Could you and your friends stop using the word *Chinaman*? Chinese people do not like that word."

"Why? A Scottish person doesn't mind if you call him a Scotsman."

"It is hard to explain. It is not the word, but the way it has been used. Chinaman's luck. Chinaman's chance. Chinky-Chinky Chinaman. When a white person says Chinaman, it is always an insult."

"What should I call you? A Celestial?"

"No. That is what newspaper reporters use when they are trying to sound sarcastic."

"Coolie?" I suggested.

"That word means 'bitter strength.' It comes from the fact we are often forced to take low-paying, dangerous jobs like railway work and tunnelling."

"What then?"

"Why do white people feel they have a right to call other people anything? Look what you see in newspapers. When they are talking about Tom Longboat, Canada's champion long-distance runner, they always call him 'The Indian.'"

"So?"

"Why do they have to mention that Longboat is an Indian?"

"It's interesting to readers. It makes him different."

"So why not talk about the white runners the same way? Next week Longboat is running against a man named Appleby. He's from England. That makes him different. Yesterday the newspaper said, 'Appleby is the Indian's greatest rival.' It should have said, 'The Englishman is the Indian's greatest rival,' or even better, 'The limey is the Indian's greatest rival.'"

I laughed. "You should be a lawyer."

"I was thinking about it, but my uncle says there is more money in dirty laundry."

"So you still haven't said what I should call you."

"Hwei."

"Just Hwei?"

"Yes. Not Hwei the Chinaman. Not Hwei the Celestial or Coolie. I'm just Hwei."

"All right, Just Hwei," I said, shaking hands. "I'll see you tomorrow."

"See you tomorrow, Just Bertie."

8

# High Tea

## January 26, 1907

We had been sailing for about two hours when Ed suddenly said, "Hey, Tommy, I've got to make a phone call."

"Right-o!" Tommy chimed.

*A phone call?* Telephones were still few and far between in Toronto. When Tommy began steering for one of the more deserted parts of the islands, I was completely mystified. The boat was still coasting to a stop when Ed jumped off the runner beam and climbed into the well-wooded shoreline.

"You're in command, Your Lordship," Tommy said to me. "I've got to make a phone call, too."

As Tommy scrambled up the bank, it suddenly occurred to me what was going on. Iceboats were wonderful inventions, but even they had their physical limitations, especially in the field of creature comforts. Between the cold, the constant bumping, and the couple of mugs of hot tea I had drunk before we had set sail that morning, I needed to pee real bad. The problem was that there weren't a whole lot of places to do it in private in the middle of a frozen lake. Especially with a female onboard.

I handed over command to Hwei, who had an urgent need, too. We left Isobel in charge, even though she was in her usual place of preference — perched in the rigging. Following Tommy's and Ed's footprints in the snow into a small gulley, Hwei and I found our crewmates competing at signing their names in a snowbank.

"Hey, Simcoe, how many *l*'s in Milwaukee?" Ed asked.

"One," I said, adding my name.

Hwei made two Chinese characters, one under the other.

"What's that?" Tommy asked.

"Hwei Coon."

We were hungry and tired. Somehow that struck us as insanely funny. We began to giggle and then laugh so hard that we almost fell down the snowbank that led back to the *Marinion*.

"Everybody make their connection all right?" Isobel asked coldly from the cockpit of the boat. Her icy tone fanned our giggle fit.

"You know, you can see more than pressure cracks from up top of that mast," she said casually.

*Oops!*

The four of us looked at one another in embarrassment. There was a short silence and then Ed said, "Hwei Coon," under his breath and we dissolved into laughter again.

Isobel shook her head impatiently and checked her pocket watch while waiting for us to get up off the ice. "I'm in the presence of idiot children."

"My ribs hurt," I complained when we were finally able to stand and think about sailing again.

"I feel like I've gone thirty rounds with Tommy Burns, the boxer," Ed admitted.

Isobel was still mad.

"We're sorry," Tommy said, trying to make amends.

"You should be," Isobel said. "Didn't it occur to any of you gentlemen that maybe I might need ... to make a phone call, too?"

To be honest, we hadn't thought about that at all. As far as we knew, women never answered the call of nature. Unlike men, they rarely mentioned the subject or even admitted they used the privy.

"The telephone's that way," Ed said, trying to keep a straight face.

"In the woods?" Isobel asked incredulously. "You expect me to ... make a phone call ... in the middle of the woods like a wild animal?"

Ed shrugged. "Well, unfortunately, there's not a whole lot of choice in the middle of the lake, especially for girls."

"Do you know where the Royal Toronto Yacht Club is?" Isobel asked Tommy.

"Sure. Are you a member?"

Isobel pointed in the direction of the club and said icily, "Isn't everybody?"

The Royal Toronto Yacht Club was one of the largest and snootiest sailing societies in Canada. It was located on the northern peninsula of the central Toronto island, and many of the city's richest bankers, businessmen, and politicians were members. The clubhouse was like a big hotel, and it even had its own fancy restaurant on the premises. Tommy had lived on the islands all his life but had never been through the front door of the club. He and his father had delivered fish to the back door many times, so he knew the maître d' very well.

His name was Mueller, but everyone called him Muley because he had big, fuzzy ears and square yellow teeth. He was always snarling at the other employees, but if he saw a club member, his face switched to a phony smile that Tommy said looked like a mule trying to hold in gas. Although he was only an employee, Muley was a bigger snob than any of the club members. He was always on the lookout for non-members attempting to use the only warm washrooms on the islands.

We pulled the *Marinion* up to the front dock and parked between two huge twin-masted ice yachts that appeared to have never been operated.

"Should we wait here?" Tommy asked.

"Of course not," Isobel said, leading the way. "You can't loiter out here. Come on."

Like a gaggle of goslings behind a mother goose, we warily followed Isobel single file up the boardwalk and steps leading to the heavy oak front doors. She paused at the entrance, and we obediently hesitated, too, until it occurred to me that she was waiting for one of us "gentlemen" to open the door for her. So I did.

"Thank you, Bertie," Isobel said regally as she glided through.

Catching on fast, Tommy and Ed nearly trampled Hwei as they stampeded forward to open the inner doors for her. They grabbed a door each so that Isobel was able to make a two-door grand entrance like visiting royalty. Heads turned in the lobby, some people smiling as they recognized Isobel in her elegant winter sailing clothes and others frowning as they noticed the small army of riff-raff in her wake.

From the doorway of the dining room, Muley locked his eyes on us in outrage. "Where do you think you're going?"

I felt my ears burn with embarrassment as every person in the lobby stared at us.

Isobel stopped like a queen about to have someone beheaded. "I'm not in the habit of informing the club staff of my itinerary."

"The restrooms are for members only," Muley said, baring his yellow teeth.

Isobel smiled coldly. "Members only ... and their guests. My father is a member of this club, and these young men are his guests. We're in the habit of washing our hands before we handle food. Am I to assume, by your remarks, that you don't follow the same philosophy?"

It was Muley's turn to redden. "No, ma'am. I mean ... yes."

"A table for five by the window when we return, please," Isobel said, resuming her journey.

We followed in silence as Isobel led us around a corner.

"Hey, there really is a telephone here," Ed said, noting a wooden box with an earphone and mouthpiece mounted on the wall.

"That's provided free for our business members," Isobel said. "Would anyone like to make a 'real' call?"

Sadly, we all shook our heads. Most of us had never actually seen a telephone before. I would have loved to call someone, but I didn't know anyone who owned a telephone.

Ed picked up the earpiece, listened, then jumped back. "Sorry!" he said to the operator, slamming the earpiece down. "It really works!"

Isobel sighed. Two wooden doors, one discreetly marked LADIES and the other GENTLEMEN were at the end of the hall. "I'll meet you back here in ten minutes," Isobel said as she strolled through the door marked LADIES.

"Ten minutes," Ed said when the door closed behind Isobel. "What's she going to do? Take a bath?"

"It always takes women longer," Hwei said. "Even in China, when a woman disappears behind a door like that, it takes ten times longer than a man."

Having recently gone, none of us really needed to pee, but we weren't going to pass up a chance to enjoy a warm restroom. We pushed on the door of the men's room and entered porcelain paradise. The Royal Toronto Yacht Club's men's room was nicer than any of the people's homes I had ever visited. The walls were solid walnut. The floor was made of brightly polished black and white tiles. There were huge silver mirrors hanging over sinks of marble with gleaming brass faucets and taps. With a whoop we peeled off our winter coats and rolled up our sleeves.

"I feel like I'm going to get arrested if I pee on this thing," Tommy said as he hovered over a spotless urinal.

"If they arrest you for that, I'll be hanged for what I'm doing in here," Ed said from inside one of the shiny wooden cubicles.

Tommy twisted a brass faucet at one of the sinks and put his hand under the spout. "Ouch! That water's hot!"

"Must be connected to a boiler somewhere," I said.

"A boiler just for hot water for the bathroom?" Tommy said.

"Gosh, these toffs have it all, don't they?" Ed added when he emerged from the wooden cubicle.

Despite several washes of soap and water, we still left about twenty yards of dark smudges on the linen roller towel before our hands were clean enough for eating. We found Isobel waiting for us as we left the men's room, watch in hand again.

"Fifteen minutes," she said, snapping her watch shut. "What were you doing in there — taking a bath?"

If we had felt conspicuous when we entered the lobby, we might as well have been Christians filing into the Roman Coliseum as we came into the dining room. A thick red Persian carpet muffled our footsteps. There were ferns and marble columns everywhere. A man in an evening suit was playing something classical on a grand piano. As a waiter led us to our table, the room went silent except for one or two forks dropping onto plates. A hundred pairs of eyes swivelled to stare at us as we crossed the room. Some people even put on their glasses to see better.

Muley appeared like a genie in a puff of smoke to pull out Isobel's chair as she sat. He made strange little kitten noises as the rest of us pulled up chairs. Then he noticed Hwei sitting between Tommy and Ed. "Miss, we're not in the habit of serving Chinamen in our dining room."

"I'm very relieved to hear that, Mr. Mueller," Isobel said. "I'm not in the habit of eating them. May I introduce you to Mr. Hwei Tai Coon of Hong Kong. His family is extensively involved in the textiles industry. You've heard of the Hong Kong Tai Coons, I hope?" She shot Muley a look that would have made a polar bear shiver.

"Oh, yes, Miss Isobel, of course," Muley lied through yellow teeth.

"Oh, good, Mr. Mueller," Isobel said. "Then you know how upset my father would be if anyone showed any disrespect for Hwei or any of his other guests."

"Yes, Miss Isobel. May I offer you all menus?" He handed out a small printed card to each of us.

"Sauerkraut juice?" Ed said, reading one of the appetizers.

"It's good for fighting scurvy," I said, alarmed to notice that most of the items had three-digit prices. Even Ed's sauerkraut juice cost more than a full lunch at Martha's Open Kitchen.

"High tea for five," Isobel said, handing the menu back without looking at it.

"High tea?" Ed asked. "How tall is high tea?"

"It's not tall," I said. "It's long. Hope you guys are hungry."

"I'm always hungry," Ed said. "How long can tea be?"

As if to answer, a cart arrived loaded with silver platters stacked with fancy sandwiches. Cups and saucers were plunked onto our table from five directions followed by individual pots of tea wrapped in hand-knitted cozies proudly bearing the RTYC initials. Four of us stared in puzzlement at the sandwiches.

"What happened to the crusts?" Ed asked.

"They cut them off," Isobel said.

"Why?" Ed asked.

Isobel sighed. "Because that's the way people like them here."

Ed shook his head. "That's all I lived on when I was a wee guy in the train yards. Maybe they cut them off here to feed orphans?"

"Possibly," Isobel said with an amused smile.

"Is there any baloney?" Tommy asked.

"None, sadly," Isobel apologized. "I believe all they have is cucumber, watercress, and butter."

"I've heard of cucumber," Tommy said. "But what's watercress?"

"I think it's a sort of lettuce that grows in rivers," Isobel said.

There was a profound silence, and all eyes turned in my direction. "Why are you guys looking at me?"

"We're waiting for you to bore us with the truth, Lord Simcoe," Ed said.

"I have no idea," I said quickly. They kept staring at me expectantly. I sighed. "Okay, watercress is a leafy member of the mustard family. The ancient Romans and Greeks both ate it, and it's also popular in China and Japan."

"Attaboy!" Tommy said as Ed and Isobel clapped.

"Did you call, Miss Isobel?" Muley asked, appearing in another puff of smoke and startling the heck out of us.

"Sorry, no ... I mean ... yes," Isobel said. "You do serve baloney, don't you?" It was a command, not a question.

"Baloney?" Muley echoed in disbelief.

"Yes, fried, please, with hot mustard and on brown bread with the crusts," Isobel said. "For two ..." she added when Ed nodded. Then she glanced inquiringly at Hwei and me.

"I'm fine with watercress and cucumber," I said, trying to impress Isobel with my manners.

"I am, too," Hwei said.

"For three then," Isobel said, smiling expectantly while Muley put on his fake smile.

"Right away, Miss Isobel," he mewed through clenched teeth.

But to give him his due, poor Muley did his duty. Hot baloney sandwiches arrived almost immediately. Hwei's and my nostrils twitched enviously as greasy garlic fumes caressed our noses. Politely, we munched delicate cold cucumber on white bread while Tommy, Ed, and Isobel happily chomped hot baloney on thickly sliced bread. Hwei and I weren't the only ones to smell the fumes. All around us plates of cucumber and watercress sandwiches were pushed aside, and demands for "The same as what those young people are having" were made. With each new baloney order, Muley's mewing became more audible.

As soon as Isobel took her last bite of baloney, our plates were whisked away from the left and fresh plates were replaced from the right. A four-storey silver tower loaded with freshly baked scones, cookies, cake slices, and fruit tarts was placed at the centre of the table. "Wow!" everyone except Isobel cried.

"How many are we allowed to take?" Tommy asked.

"As many as you like," Isobel said.

"Wow!" we all said again. I chose two slices of Black Forest chocolate cake and a raspberry tart.

"Hey, this cream's gone bad!" Ed said, tilting a bowl of thick white liquid in his hand. "It's lumpy."

"That's clotted cream," I said. "It's supposed to be that way. It goes on your scones or tarts."

"Really?" he said, happily pouring half the bowl over one scone. Then he bit down with delight. "Hey, it's good!"

As stuffed as I was, I knew it would be a long time before I likely tasted chocolate again, so I helped myself to a third piece of Black Forest cake, even though my stomach was already complaining. As usual Tommy and Ed were smarter. They skimmed a half-dozen desserts each into napkins, which they transferred to their coat pockets for later eating.

As soon as Isobel folded her napkin, Muley appeared in a final puff of smoke and presented her with a chit to sign. For the first time since we had walked through the door, he seemed happy. Isobel signed the chit with her initials.

"Thank you, Miss Isobel," Muley said as we stood.

"By the way," Isobel asked as we headed for the front door, "would it be all right if I brought my parents down for a ride on the *Marinion* next Saturday? They're a little concerned about the reports they've been getting from Fräulein von Tirpitz, so the best remedy, I think, is to give them a demonstration of how safe iceboat sailing is."

Tommy and Ed suddenly looked worried.

"Sure," Tommy said. As rocky as the recruitment process had been at the beginning, I could tell he was now afraid of losing Isobel as a crew member. It wasn't just her sailing skills. We were still two crew members short for the big February race.

"And the rest of you must come, too," Isobel said. That wasn't an invitation. It was a command performance. As afraid as we were of making fools of ourselves in front of her parents, we couldn't say no after the big meal she had bought us.

"Sure," Tommy said.

"Yeah," Ed agreed.

"I'm delighted," I said, trying to sound confident.

As we left the dining room, orders for hot baloney were still ringing out.

"I don't think this dining room will ever be quite the same," Isobel said as mewing Muley rushed by with three more baloney sandwiches.

9

# Groundhog Day

## February 2, 1907

Without being told, Hwei and I showed up early the next Saturday to make sure everything was shipshape on the *Marinion* before Isobel arrived with her family. I had even borrowed some nice cushions from our parlour for the DeSalle family to sit on, and Tommy had scrounged the cleanest-looking buffalo robes from the other boat skippers. It was an overcast day with a gusting wind, which would make the sailing interesting.

"Let's just keep the speed low and at no time let the *Marinion* hike," Tommy said in our strategy huddle.

"Here they come," Hwei said.

The DeSalles' teal blue Rolls-Royce limousine had just parked at the foot of York Street. A chauffeur in a matching blue uniform complete with brown leather gauntlets and knee-high riding boots swung out of the open driver's seat on the right-hand side and scurried to the enclosed cab at the back. Coming to attention, he opened the door and stood back. One by one the DeSalle family exited, starting with Isobel's father.

Even though he was shorter than average, Mr. DeSalle seemed to radiate authority. As he stepped forward, people naturally got out of his way or tipped their hats to him. Mrs. DeSalle was so wrapped up for the weather that only the bottom half of her face showed below a big hat tied under her chin with a silk scarf. Even like that she turned men's heads in admiration and women's heads in jealousy as she walked arm in arm with her husband. Isobel cantered behind in her racing clothes, and Fräulein von Tirpitz brought up the rear. As usual the Fräulein looked ready to do battle.

"There zey are," von Tirpitz said, pointing at us as if she were picking murder suspects out of a police lineup.

Isobel introduced us, and Mr. DeSalle pumped our hands one by one. He seemed genuinely happy to meet us. "Both Isobel and Fräulein von Tirpitz have told us so much about you."

"And which one do you believe?" Ed asked mischievously, which made Mrs. DeSalle smile and her husband laugh.

Fräulein von Tirpitz's head kept swivelling as if she were searching for exactly the right yardarm to hang us from.

"So you're Isobel's skipper," Mr. DeSalle said as he released Tommy's hand.

"Yes, sir."

"It's very generous of you to allow her to be part of your crew," Mr. DeSalle said. "Most sailing men are rather traditional in their views about not allowing women aboard their vessels."

"Hey, it's 1907," Ed said. "You gotta move with the times."

"Women will want to vote next," von Tirpitz said with a grimace.

Tommy led everyone over to the *Marinion.*

"It's an unusual name," Mr. DeSalle commented.

"It was my grandmother's maiden name," Tommy said.

"It's also the name of a type of fish found in the Caribbean," I said. "It belongs to the order of sawbellies."

Everyone paused and stared at me.

"Don't mind him," Ed apologized. "He reads books."

Like Isobel, Mr. DeSalle seemed to know more about the *Marinion*'s rigging than even Tommy did. "These sails can be dropped almost instantly. I imagine that comes in handy if you suddenly see a wide expanse of open water in front of you."

"Yes, or if something unwanted suddenly gets caught in your rigging," Tommy said, glancing at Isobel.

"Did we come here to talk or sail?" Isobel demanded.

Mr. DeSalle laughed as we swung the *Marinion* into launch position. "Always to the point, that girl." After securely seating the DeSalles and Fräulein von Tirpitz in the cockpit, we took up our starting posts. To balance our uneven strengths, Hwei and I took the weatherly beam while Ed and Isobel took the lee.

"Ready!" Tommy said.

"Ready!" we all responded.

"Launch!"

Mr. DeSalle watched with approval as we shoved off in one easy motion. Tommy hauled back on the halyard, and the *Marinion*'s old parchment-coloured sail rose smoothly and caught the wind. We swung aboard and hauled in the sail to catch enough of the wind to bring us up to twenty miles per hour. With this wind we could have easily done twice that speed, but Tommy wanted to impress the DeSalles with how safe iceboating was. Fortunately, there were no other boats out at the moment racing or pulling stunts.

To my surprise, neither Mrs. DeSalle nor Fräulein von Tirpitz seemed the least bit frightened.

"Are you okay?" Ed asked Mrs. DeSalle.

"Very well, thank you," she said with just the faintest French accent. "Like Isobel, I've been on sailboats all my life."

"And Fräulein von Tirpitz comes from a famous German sailing family," Mr. DeSalle said. "Her uncle's a high-ranking admiral in the Imperial German Navy."

"And is she visiting you for long?" Tommy asked.

"No," the Fräulein said. "I am here to teach Miss Dezalle ze proper way to be a young lady."

*"Hooooooeeeeeeee!"* Isobel cried from the topmast. She had climbed up there against Tommy's orders, and if his eyes had been a bird gun, he would have given her both barrels.

"Isobel!" Mrs. DeSalle shouted in alarm. "What on earth are you doing up there?"

"You zee?" Fräulein von Tirpitz crowed in triumph. "That iz what I was telling you about! She climbz up like a monkey, *ja*?"

"Deadhead one hundred yards," Isobel warned. "Clear ice ten degrees to starboard."

"Ten degrees starboard," Tommy echoed. The *Marinion*'s bow turned, and the deadhead shot past on the port runner.

"I didn't know iceboats used lookouts," Mr. DeSalle said, impressed.

"Most don't," Tommy said. "We're one of the first."

Mr. DeSalle nodded. "A splendid idea, especially out here where things can happen so fast."

We cruised along the shoreline and pretended to race a chugging old freight train. A small boy on a decent bicycle could have beat either one of us, but the DeSalles and the Fräulein became caught up in the excitement as we slowly crept along.

"We won!" von Tirpitz exclaimed as we finally inched ahead of the locomotive, her sailing blood clearly beginning to take over.

With the Western Gap coming up, Tommy made a gentle turn so we could skirt the shorelines of the islands. We entered Blockhouse Bay between Hanlan's Point and Mugg's Island.

"So pretty," Mrs. DeSalle said.

Snow had fallen overnight, and many of the willows were still clad in a fresh layer of white. At this speed Tommy was able to dodge in an out of some of the smaller channels between the islands.

"Oh, do be careful!" Fräulein von Tirpitz cried when Ed leaned out from the shroud line and casually snapped a wind-dried cattail head off as we passed close to the shore.

"A winter bloom for a beautiful lady," Ed said, offering von Tirpitz the cattail head with a bow.

The Fräulein accepted the gift with a blush.

I wondered where Ed had learned to do that and made a mental note to remember how he had done it. What was it with women and flowers, anyway?

Once we were back out in the bay, Tommy gave Mr. DeSalle a chance to steer. He took to it as if he had been doing it all his life. We circled the bay twice more, with Isobel and her mother steering. Even Fräulein von Tirpitz agreed to try when Ed offered to share the tiller with her.

Before we knew it two hours had passed. Suddenly, we noticed we were chilled and hungry.

"I have an idea," Mr. DeSalle said. "Let's go to the yacht club for lunch. Our treat for the boat ride."

We didn't need to be asked twice.

As we entered the dining room, Muley turned, took one look at us, and yelped as if he had been kicked in the pants.

"Sorry to startle you, Mr. Mueller," Mr. DeSalle said. "Table for eight, please."

Muley sat us down.

"Doez anyone else hear a kitten in here?" Fräulein von Tirpitz asked as Muley circled behind us. She made sure she sat next to Ed.

"Fried baloney sandwiches," Mrs. DeSalle said, glancing at the specials of the day. "How unusual."

"I hear they're quite good here," Isobel said, smiling.

After lunch we ferried the DeSalles and Fräulein von Tirpitz back to York Street. Walking them up to their car, we caught the chauffeur, hat off, trying to impress a couple of shop girls from Simpson's Department Store by letting them sit in the front of the limousine.

*"Achtung!"* Fräulein von Tirpitz cried, clearing her throat.

The chauffeur banged his head when he jumped out of the Rolls-Royce and jammed his hat on crooked while coming to attention. The shop girls slid discreetly out of the vehicle on the far side and slunk away, giggling.

"Men!" the Fräulein muttered in disgust. "But not you, Edward," she added, touching Ed's hand as the red-faced chauffeur assisted Mrs. DeSalle into the warm, enclosed cab.

"The redhead was a looker, James," Mr. DeSalle commented to his driver, climbing into the car.

Mrs. DeSalle and the Fräulein were going shopping at Eaton's. Mr. DeSalle was heading to the Toronto Club. The good news was that Isobel was allowed to stay with us for some more sailing practice. Reluctantly, Fräulein von Tirpitz took her leave of Ed. She gave him a firm Prussian handshake, then clanked into the back of the car.

"You dog you," Tommy said to Ed, giving his arm a punch as the Rolls-Royce rumbled away.

"She's not so bad once you get her to smile," Ed said.

"Her uncle's very protective," Isobel warned.

Tommy laughed. "Great! If he hears about you, we'll have to outrun a German man-o-war."

"Dreadnought," I corrected.

"I won't," Ed said.

I almost opened my mouth to explain that the German Navy was now comprised of battleships called dreadnoughts but changed my mind. We had things to do.

---

"You guys are nuts!"

"We prefer the term *crazy*," Ed said as two potential recruits bailed off the *Marinion* even before we came to a halt.

They hit the ice and rolled for five yards. As soon as they could get back on their feet, they scuttled for the shore, firing back rude insults and gestures at us.

"Anyone else?" Tommy asked, scanning the shoreline.

"Nope," Ed said. "That's the last of them."

It was getting late in the season. Today was Groundhog Day. Whether the varmint's predictions were true or not, the ice could conceivably be gone in a few more weeks and we were still short two crew members. Tommy and Ed had put up notices in the local factories and warehouses advertising for teenage ice sailing recruits. Ten brave-looking young men had responded. None had made the grade.

"Well, we're still two crewmen short," Tommy said.

"We may be shorter than that," Hwei said, pointing with his chin at the shoreline.

About a hundred yards away, standing behind a cart load of coal, was Mr. DeSalle. He was watching us through a small pair of binoculars. Obviously, he had seen what the *Marinion* could really do. Mr. DeSalle knew he had been spotted. With a slightly embarrassed smile he put away the binoculars and approached us.

"The jig's up," Ed moaned.

"Things were kind of dead at the club, so I'd thought I'd come back down here," Mr. DeSalle explained. "Is it my imagination or did you give a slightly different kind of ride for those gentlemen?"

"Wind picked up a bit," Ed said.

"And your boat's routinely capable of those speeds?"

"Even more if the wind's right," Tommy said.

Mr. DeSalle climbed into the *Marinion*. "Right. Let's have a real ride then."

# 10

# The Thaw

## February 9, 1907

"No sailing today," Tommy said as I walked out to the *Marinion* the following Saturday.

"Why not?"

"Too warm."

I understood. The previous Sunday a freak thaw had warmed the ice all week.

"Look out there!" Tommy suddenly yelled.

I followed his pointing finger and spotted several men standing around a stranded iceboat.

"That guy decided to try, anyway," Tommy said. "Now he's got a runner sunk through the ice."

"Anyone go in?" I asked.

Tommy shook his head. "No, but one of his crew broke his front teeth on the bow when that thing came to a sudden halt from thirty miles an hour. He also broke his runner. I don't want to risk our boat or crew. We're too close to the big race."

I was disappointed, but I could see Tommy's point.

Hwei and Isobel had already come and gone. I hung around with Tommy and Ed for a quick tea and tattie, then decided to head home and get a jump on my English composition assignment. Miss Worthington had asked us to write a thousand-word essay about the wonder of nature, and I was writing about how man-made objects like iceboats became beautiful works of art with just the addition of wind.

The walking was tough going. I had mistakenly taken a shortcut by going diagonally across the ice to John Street, but the ice there was so rotten that my feet kept breaking through the upper crust. My boots were soaked and my feet kept sliding off at different angles. I was relieved when I had only another hundred feet to go before I hit dry land. Putting my head down, I hunkered forward only to bump against something unexpectedly.

It was a solid wall of Kellys!

"Hello, McCross," Sean said. "Thought we'd forgotten you?"

"I'm not selling papers anymore, Sean," I said. "We have no quarrel." I stepped back and almost fell in the wet snow. The Kellys circled me like a human cage.

"True," Sean said, "but you still owe us for December's back rent, not to mention the ten days I spent in jail over the Christmas holidays."

"You?" I said. "I saw you get away clean."

"I did, but I wasn't going to let my clan get locked up by themselves, was I? Ever spend a night as a guest of the city, McCross?"

"No."

Sean shot me an almost friendly smile. "It's an eye-opener for sure. There are some very bad people in there, and a small boy like Liam could get hurt really bad. And the bulls don't care what happens once they close that door. I had to get myself arrested because of you. Like I said, you owe me ten dollars for December and ten days for my time in the clink. But I bet you think you don't have the money or the time, right, McCross?"

I shook my head.

Sean nodded to his gang. "I thought so. In that case we'll have to settle for your lousy hide."

Before Sean or his gang could do anything, I was already heading straight for the weakest point in the circle — Hughie. I had noticed that while Sean was talking to me Hughie was doing his usual impression of a window dummy. The warm weather and Sean's chit-chat had almost lulled him into sleeping on his feet. Lunging forward, I used the crown of my bowler hat as a battering ram, hitting Hughie square under the chin. He landed with a wet splat, and I treated his chest and face as starting blocks to get a good head start on his relatives.

I had two advantages over the Kellys. One, they were all wearing smooth-soled landlubber winter boots that were the worst things to have on when dealing with wet ice. Second, one skill I had learned over the past month or so was how to read ice. Slightly off to my left was a big square patch of ice that was faintly darker than the rest of the bay. Judging by the regular shape of that area, it was obvious that ice men had been working there recently. At least it was apparent to me, but I was pretty sure the Kellys wouldn't know about it.

I skirted the dark patch on the left and then cut right so the Kellys would race straight over the thin ice to cut me off. When a few of the smallest, lightest Kellys crossed the patch without incident, I began to worry, but suddenly there was a satisfying crack and splash. I glanced back and saw several Kellys flailing in the water. No one was chasing me now, so I slowed to a walk. Sean had managed to stay dry, but he was having a hard time getting to his gang because the ice was now fracturing in all directions like a broken window.

"Come on!" Sean bellowed at the kids in the water. "Get out of there!"

"We can't!" they screamed as they floundered. "It's too slippery!" More Kellys fell in, trying to pull their brothers and cousins out.

"Hold on!" Sean yelled, running toward the hole. "I'm coming!"

I told myself to head for shore then, unbelievably, my legs mutinied again. Instead of running away from the Kellys, I was hurtling toward them. "Wait, you stupid dolt!" I shouted at Sean. The way he was charging forward he was going to make matters worse. I was right. Sean went crashing through the ice and opened up a space big enough to bring down three more Kellys. Nine of the twelve Kellys were in the water now.

"Something's pulling on my legs!" someone cried.

Likely, there was a current there, I thought. I ordered my legs to turn around, but they kept pumping toward the hole. The Kellys were in serious trouble.

"Get a rope!" Sean ordered Hughie, who was standing with his mouth wide open.

"There's no time," I said. "Hughie, lie down on the ice."

"I just got up," he growled sullenly, raising his hands pug-style as if he now wanted to fight.

"Lie down, you big oaf!" I hollered.

"Do it, Hughie!" Sean ordered, and Hughie lay down.

"You, with the ears," I said to a tall, gangly Kelly with two huge lugs, "lie down in front of Hughie. And you, Hughie, lock your arms around his legs."

One by one I organized the Kellys in a human chain the way Tommy and Ed had shown me. Only this time it was me at the end of a chain of Kellys.

The closer we got to the hole the more the ice cracked and sank menacingly. I couldn't believe I was doing this for the Kellys, but my head was no longer in control.

*"Hiiieee!"* I couldn't help yelping as frigid water seeped into my pants. Taking off my bowler, I could just reach the edge of the hole. Several pairs of hands grasped frantically at my hat. "One at a time or you'll drown us all!" I yelled.

"Listen to him," Sean said, using his free hand to cudgel his gang into line. "Joseph, you first."

"Take your time!" I cautioned. "Easy!" Joseph grabbed my hat, then my hand, and then hauled himself up my arm and down my back. "Don't stand. Just pull yourself along to the end as if we're a ladder." As soon as I felt Joseph move off my legs, I shouted, "Next!"

"Matthew!" Sean ordered, and the next Kelly repeated the process.

About four Kellys later I noticed that the water was no longer just up to my midsection. It was past my boots!

"I think this ice won't hold out much longer," I said quietly to Sean.

He nodded and kept making his selections based on who looked most like they were about to drown.

I heard Ed's and Tommy's voices somewhere behind me. A rope end hit the water, and Sean caught it. There were just two Kellys left in the ice now — Sean and his brother, Liam. The opposite of Sean, Liam was the family runt. Even in winter clothes he seemed almost half his twelve years. Still, he was as wiry as an alley rat. I felt his hands latch onto my coat sleeves as he heaved himself up and forward. Sean was being pulled out with the rope.

"Made it," I whispered.

And then we were gone.

Before either of us knew what was happening, the ice gave way and Liam and I tumbled into the water. The shock of plunging into a frozen lake was unbelievable — now I knew how a crab felt being scalded alive in a pot. I forced my eyes open and discovered that Liam and I were at least six feet from the nearest edge of the hole. Our combined weight had dragged us down, the current had caught us, and we were being slowly drawn out to deeper water.

My first urge was to shake Liam off my back. I knew there was no way I could swim with him holding on. Unfortunately, my body was still in mutiny mode, though, so he stayed.

A big bubble of air had been trapped under my leather coat. It acted like a float and pulled us belly up toward the surface. As soon as we touched the underside of the ice, I tried to get a handhold, but it was too slippery. Every second, we were being pushed farther and father from the opening. My air was running out. I could already imagine the sharp bite of the Harbour Patrol's grappling hooks fishing me out in the springtime, with little Liam Kelly still clasped like a barnacle to my cold dead butt.

Then something tapping caught my attention. Silhouetted against the ice above were Ed's ice picks, which had escaped from my sleeves. They were meant for pulling people over the top of ice, but there was no reason they couldn't work upside down.

The tops had already floated off as I grabbed each pick. I punched the right one into the ice, and we stopped moving downstream. I jabbed the left one in, pulled hard, and we glided forward. It was working!

Through the ice I heard loud pounding and actually saw feet passing inches from my face on the ice above. Voices shouted. I crawled toward the light, but I was running out of oxygen. My head began to throb as something tried to break its way out of my skull from the inside.

I used the sound of Sean's big mouth to guide me toward the hole. It had to be close. More sunlight seemed to be getting through. A thin bubble of air escaped my nose, carrying a spiderweb of red goo, and I realized that the blood vessels in my sinuses were bursting. But we were so close now. Maybe a half-dozen feet. But my legs were numb from the cold, and I couldn't feel the ice picks in my hands anymore. My lungs were about to burst. I tried to lessen the pressure by letting out a little air. Bad mistake. As soon as I loosened my grip a little, my lungs wouldn't listen to reason. They pushed out all the air and they inhaled. Greedy things.

Ice-cold water blasted into my lungs, making me cough, sputter, and shake like a wild animal caught in a trap. Liam's arms clenched even tighter around my neck. I realized with a pang that it was my fault he was down here. *Sorry, Liam, you repulsive little man. Even though you're a Kelly, I had no right to kill you.* As light faded to dark, I reached up and gave one of his tiny rat claws a goodbye squeeze.

I had been told that drowning was the most pleasant way to die. That turned out to be an outright lie. I had also been told that before you died you got to see a short summary of your life like one of those moving pictures I still hadn't seen yet. Lie number two. The last thing I saw before I died was Sean Kelly's ugly mug. His thick red hair floated like a halo over his round white face. A dark tunnel seemed to close around him until I could only see his pale blue eyes staring at me as he watched me die. The world turned black. I felt my feet touch the bottom of the lake, and then I was gone.

Bees. Thousands of buzzing bees were crawling all over me. Their wings were making an incessant drone. They were stinging me. My whole body was on fire with bee stings. I opened my eyes and felt light stab into them.

"Look," a voice said, "he's opening his eyes."

"Call the nurse," someone else said. It sounded like Tommy.

Several sets of booted feet ran down the wooden hallway while I struggled to focus my eyes and sit up.

"Stay down, McCross. Don't strain yourself," yet another voice said as a strong hand pushed me back onto the pillow. If I hadn't known better, I would have sworn it was Sean.

The army of boots returned, along with the smell of antiseptic. "Yes, he's waking," a female voice said.

I could now make out blurs all around me. There was silence for about thirty seconds until, one at a time, my eyes focused and I found myself lying in a white metal bed surrounded by Kellys. Fortunately, Tommy and Ed plus a nurse were there, so they couldn't kill me, at least not yet. I couldn't talk. A thick, metallic taste filled my mouth, and my tongue was covered in fur.

"Give him a drink of water," a Kelly suggested.

"The last thing I want is more water," I croaked, and everyone laughed, even the nurse.

"He climbs Christmas trees, he goes ice bathing, and he returns from the dead," Tommy said. "There's no end to this boy's talents."

"You really had us worried," Ed said.

Tommy grinned. "Yeah, where would we find another crazy rig rat this close to the end of the season?"

"What happened?" I asked.

"First, you saved a dozen Kellys, then Sean pulled you and Liam out of the lake," Ed said. "Liam shook it off like a collie dog, but you've been out for the past forty-eight hours. We pumped half the lake out of your lungs, but you caught a fever. Probably more from drinking that sewer water than from the ice bath. I told you to keep your mouth shut."

"Everything hurts," I wailed. "Especially my feet."

"Oh, they had to amputate them," Ed said quietly. "Frostbite."

"What!" I cried, sitting up and grabbing my feet which, though they hurt like heck, were definitely still attached to me.

Tommy and Ed keeled over. That was the funniest joke they had pulled yet. They were laughing so hard they failed to notice that someone else had entered the room. It looked like a circus weightlifter dolled up in a woman's wig and dress. Ringlets of red hair streaked with grey escaped from a huge hat sporting a dead rabbit as a centrepiece. The head beneath featured a massive square jaw sitting on two enormous shoulders and a huge bosom thrusting straight out like an advancing thundercloud.

Before Tommy and Ed knew what was happening, the stranger threw a brawny arm around each of them and, without straining, lifted them off the floor. "Are these the heroes who saved my little Liam?" she asked huskily.

"They're his friends, Ma," Sean Kelly said. "That's your hero in bed there."

Still clutching Tommy and Ed to her chest like rag dolls, Mrs. Kelly leaned over the bed and planted a big, wet kiss on my forehead. "Ah, thank God you were on the ice when my little Liam fell through. It was the Lord's sweet mercy to put you there in that exact spot. Sean told me how you organized the rescue brigade and almost lost your own life savin' others."

Still locked in Mrs. Kelly's arms, Ed and Tommy were slowly turning blue.

"Ma, I think you're crushing them," little Liam said

from below. He had been clinging to his mother's leg the whole time. Now I knew where he had learned to hang on so well.

"Sorry, boys," Mrs. Kelly said, finally releasing Tommy and Ed, who fell away like two sacks of straw. Both took a huge gasp of air. "I get passionate sometimes. I'm just a poor frail woman, you know."

"Yeah, Ma," the Kelly boys all said together.

Mercifully, the nurse made sure the Kelly visit was short. "He needs his rest," she said, motioning the Kelly kids out and edging Mrs. Kelly through the doorway like a tiny tug nudging an ocean liner. "You other boys, too," she said, pointing at Ed, Tommy, and Sean.

"I need just one more minute — alone," Sean said.

Great, in my current condition all he needed was two seconds to kill me and he'd still have fifty-eight more to make his getaway.

"All right," the nurse said. "You were the one who pulled him out of the water, so you deserve one minute. That way Mr. McCross can properly thank you for saving his life."

*Me thanking Sean for saving my life?* So this was hell. The sound of feet receded down the hall, and then it was just me and Sean.

He stared at me for half a minute as if he were lost for words. He opened his mouth twice to say something, then shut it again. Finally, he asked in a soft voice, "So why'd you come back? You had a clean getaway and we'd likely all be dead."

The smart thing to do at that point would have been to make up some grand motive of the brotherhood of mankind, being a good Canadian, doing the right thing, that kind of hogwash. "I don't know," I said. "I honestly don't. I just did it. So why'd you pull me out?"

Sean thought that over for a moment, then said with a straight face. "I didn't. I couldn't get Liam to let go of you, so I had to pull you both out."

I grinned.

Sean stuck out his hand. "Good enough."

"Good enough," I echoed, then drifted off to sleep with the sound of bees still buzzing in my ears.

---

After another day in the hospital, I was allowed to go home. My mother had arranged with our neighbour, Mr. Hacker the knacker, to bring me home in his cart. Two dead sheep and a drowned pig were piled in the back of the wagon. "Glad you're still able to sit at the front of the wagon, boy," Mr. Hacker said as I shivered under a double buffalo robe. The minute I arrived Mom put me straight to bed.

"I'll make you some soup," she promised, which made me shiver even worse. But before she could, there was a knock at the door and I heard her talking to someone. My mother sounded surprised, but I heard her say thank-you. Five minutes later Mom arrived with a steaming bowl of liquid. "Mr. Coon, the laundryman, sent this over for you. Silken chicken soup, he said."

For some reason the chicken was black, but it tasted wonderful. My shivering stopped and the fever went down. I fell asleep only to hear someone knocking at the door again. This time my father answered. Judging by the accent of the visitor, I was sure it was a Kelly, but I couldn't tell which one.

"Yes?" Father asked.

"Me ma wants Bertie and his friends to come to dinner next Saturday," the Kelly said.

To my horror, I heard my father say, "Why, I'm sure they'd be delighted."

"Here's our address. Are you okay, mister?"

"Why, yes, son. Why?"

"Looks like you're crying."

"It's the smell of the factory next door."

"I don't smell nothin'"

"You're very lucky then, son."

# 11

# Cork Town

**February 16, 1907**

"Parliament Street," the driver drawled in a bored voice as the Queen Street tram slowed to a stop. Tommy, Ed, and I stepped down onto a slanted wooden sidewalk that seemed to be disintegrating into the road.

"Okay, which way?" Tommy asked.

Ed checked the directions the Kelly had dropped off. "One block east on Queen and two blocks south on Power Street."

Ed and Tommy took a bearing from the Metropolitan Methodist Cathedral spire in the west to determine the right direction.

"That way," Tommy said, and we started picking our way east.

Normally, after a full day's sailing, we would have been glad to be invited to a hot meal, but dinner at the Kellys was a bit daunting. We had to step carefully. Working streetlights in this part of town were few, and many boards on the sidewalk were broken or missing altogether. We were going even slower because every few steps Ed stopped and examined his shoes.

"What?" Tommy asked finally.

"I think I stepped in something," Ed said. "I can smell it, but I can't see anything."

We all studied Ed's shoes. They looked clean.

Tommy took a deep breath and wrinkled his nose. "I think it's this whole neighbourhood. What's that smell?"

"Some old geezer's armpit," Ed suggested.

"Rotting garbage?" I said.

"Something dead?" Tommy threw out.

"All of the above," we all agreed.

If I had thought the buildings in my neighbourhood were rundown and shabby, I had never seen anything like the Kelly neighbourhood that was known as Cork Town. It was just south of Cabbagetown, one of the worst Protestant slums in the British Empire. Cabbagetown had gotten its name because the local inhabitants were so poor they grew cabbages in both their front and back yards just to have enough to eat and survive. Cork Town was equally poor, the difference being that most of its inhabitants were Irish Catholics who were even farther down Canada's social ladder. Opinions were divided as to where Cork Town had derived its moniker. Some said it had come from the fact that so many people living in the district were from a place called Cork in Ireland. Others claimed it was from the fact that there were so many shabby bars in the area.

We came to the first corner. "Wow!" Ed said, pointing at a beautiful new building made of ornately carved pink and purple stone. "Look at that!"

"That's St. Paul's Roman Catholic Church," Tommy said. "It's one of our landmarks."

We turned right, and the sidewalks and buildings got progressively scruffier except for a huge four-storey structure surrounded by a big lawn and iron gates. "House of Providence," Tommy read from a sign at the gate.

"Is that where the priests live?" Ed asked, whistling.

"No, House of Providence is a euphemism for nuthouse," I said.

"I know what a nuthouse is," Ed said. "But what's a euphemism?"

The street was supposed to be paved, but most of the cobblestones had long disappeared, leaving behind only loose dirt. Wagon ruts and potholes the size of bathtubs cratered the surface as if an artillery barrage had just landed. Electricity poles leaned at crazy angles.

It was hard to tell where one house began and the other ended because they were crowded so close together and made from the same scavenged materials. And over and over again the stink rose and sank but never left our nostrils completely.

"I wouldn't keep chickens in that wreck," Tommy said of a house to our left.

"Its neighbour looks worse," I said.

Something very large snuffled and growled as it kept pace with us on the other side of an unpainted board fence. I put my face close to a crack in the boards to try to see what it was, and the fence shuddered as something slammed itself against the boards with a vicious snarl. A shrill female voice called from the other side of the fence. "Pay-ter! Pay-ter. Quit making that racket. Get back to your shed. Go on now." The creature growled again and reluctantly moved away from the fence.

"Pay-ter?" Tommy said. "Was that a person or an animal?"

"Don't know," I said. "Don't care as long as it stays on that side of the fence." My breath was just coming back after my heart nearly jumped out of my throat. Then we came to another cross street.

"Okay, this is King Street," Tommy said. "Now we turn left."

We walked for two minutes, then turned one last time up a little lane called Wilkins.

Ed frowned. "Now there are no house numbers."

"The note says to look for a house with green shingles," Tommy said.

"They all look green — with moss," I said.

We were on the verge of turning around and making a run for it when a voice said, "Ho! Boyos. Over here!" It was Hammy standing across the street in front of a laneway that smelled strongly of livestock.

Reluctantly, we crossed over.

"Ma thought you might have a hard time finding us, being your first time in town and all," Hammy said.

"It is a little confusing," I admitted.

"No worry," Hammy said. "This way. Mind the turdie piles." He led us down a winding path littered with animal waste of nearly every description.

"I smell animals, but I don't see any," I said to Hammy.

"Animals don't last long here. They brings them in and we eats them. Nothing left but their turdies. Can't use the turdies."

"How's the arm?" I asked, then felt like kicking myself

for reminding Hammy about our porcupine dance.

"All healed," he said proudly, pulling back his coat sleeve to show me. "Ma had some job pulling out all those needles, but once she put some of her pig fat salve on me arm it healed up right fine."

There was absolutely no malice in his voice, which was the essence of a Kelly. You were either a friend or an enemy with no ground between.

Hammy turned left, and we walked the last twenty yards across a dirt yard in near-perfect darkness. The only light visible was from a small window that lit the way to the foundation of what appeared to have been a once-grand home. The upper floors were missing, but a set of stone steps led down to a basement door.

Hammy threw open the door, and the darkness and cold of a Cork Town winter evening disappeared in a blast of light and heat. "Ma, we're here!" he said, leading the way into the kitchen, which seemed to take up the whole basement.

Mrs. Kelly stood in front of a massive wood stove that strained under the weight of nearly a dozen iron and copper cauldrons of different sizes. Sheets and long johns hung in rows from the heavy, rough-hewn beams in the ceiling. "Ah, there you are at last!" she cried, picking up Tom, Ed, and me in a single hug.

Our feet didn't touch the ground for a full minute while she again thanked God we had been put there on the lake that very day to rescue her little boy from the devil's icy clutches of the lake. I relived my drowning experience as the air was slowly squeezed from my lungs. Just before I passed out we were released. On the way over I had wondered how much she knew about my part in putting her little boy and all his siblings into those icy clutches, but apparently Sean hadn't said a word.

Mrs. Kelly was the mirror image of her son, Sean, and of Liam, and of every Kelly, whether he was short, tall, hairy, scary, big, or small. There were also a half-dozen young female Kellys I had never known existed helping their mother cook and do laundry. Big, tall, thin, small, and yet they all exactly resembled their mother without duplicating one another. It was amazing!

We were given the chairs of honour near the fireplace. I sat across from Tommy and Ed and was handed a cup of tea by a beaming little Kelly girl. "I got no teeth!" she exclaimed proudly.

"Sean tells me you were in the newspaper business like himself," Mrs. Kelly said as she stirred a huge cauldron with a spoon the size of a canoe paddle.

"The newspaper business?" I glanced at Sean, and for the first time I saw fear in his eyes. "Oh, yes, newspapers. Yes, I was."

"Ah, 'tis hard work that. Long hours, and those blaggardin' bulls are always pickin' on me poor Sean. Do you know they had the audacity to arrest him and half me boys on Christmas Eve?"

"Really?" I said.

"Kept them there until Epiphany. It banjanxed the whole holiday. Me and the girls were here waitin' for Sean and the boys to come home so we could go to Christmas Eve Mass. Sean sings solo in the choir, you know."

"Really?" I repeated, giving Sean a surprised look.

"Aw, Ma," he said as he dropped his eyes like a shy shop girl.

"Ah, he sings like the angel he is. Father Thomas was heartbroken when we had to tell him Sean wasn't comin' to Mass due to a family emergency. Then we all had to walk forty-five minutes to the police station because the streetcars were jammed with drunks on Christmas Eve. The desk sergeant was an awful Neddy. Treated us like boggers. I says, 'We may be poor, but we're hard-working folk just tryin' to make a livin'.' Then he gives me some mongo sap story about Sean and the boys tearin' up the whole market tryin' to murder some little ratbark who started the whole thing by attackin' Hammy and Hughie. Show him your arms, boyos."

Hammy and Hughie held up their arms.

"Sean said he and the boys were shoppin' for presents when this little pikey ups and bashes them with a pair of — what were those hellish creatures called, Sean?"

"Porkerpines, Ma."

Mrs. Kelly scowled. "Porkerpines! What kind of country is this where pigs wear pin coats? And what kind of mucksavage would attack a group of peace-lovin' lads with a pair of porkerpines on their way to Christmas Eve Mass?"

"Terrible," Tommy said.

"Must have been insane," Ed agreed with a straight face.

"Well, he wasn't the only eedgit loose that night, because instead of arrestin' him, the bulls arrested me darlin' Sean and his lads."

"That's awful!" Tommy said.

"And there were me and the girls standin' in the police station and bein' jostled by harlots and hoodlums and bein' told that me own honest lads would have to stay in jail until they went before a magistrate who didn't drop his fat behind on his high and mighty bench until December 27. And after that the wig gave them ten days in jail because they couldn't pay the fine."

Ed rolled his eyes in sympathy. "That's horrible!"

While she was talking Mrs. Kelly was lifting the lids on various cauldrons and, with a long pair of tongs, alternately inspecting the contents of each pot. She extracted sheets, potatoes, socks and cabbages as she worked her way around the stove. The last thing she removed with a pair of iron tongs was a whole sheep's head with a big gash down the middle. The hot broth had caused the lips to peel back so that its white teeth showed in a phoney grin just like Muley's. In the dim light the head seemed to look directly at me, and I could have sworn it gave me a wink.

"If I ever find that pin-pig padjo, I'll give him what-for," she said, crushing the skull with a snap of her tongs. Suddenly, a worried look crossed her face. "You boys like mutton, I hope."

"Oh, yes, ma'am!" Tom, Ed, and I said in unison.

"Good. Beak's nearly ready. Take your places, boys."

As we moved toward the dinner table, which consisted of several small tables joined together and covered with three patched but clean tablecloths, I noticed a photograph on the wall with a lit candle in front of it. "Who's that?" I asked.

"Da," one of the Kelly girls said quietly.

After an awkward pause, Sean filled in the rest. "Father

was a teamster, a wagon driver who could handle up to a dozen horses in a single rig. A few years ago, when jobs were scarce in Toronto, he signed on to haul supplies when our soldiers went to Africa to fight the Boers."

"Was he killed?" I asked.

"We don't know. He just never came back. The Boers had German cannons that could throw bombs miles behind the British lines. One day the Boer shells hit Da's camp. They found his wagon with the horses still hitched, but no trace of him. Only shell holes."

"The army said he ran away," Liam added. "That's why we didn't get a pension. But Da never ran away from anything."

"Even if he did, he'd be back here by now," Molly said. "There's no way he'd abandon us."

"He's dead and they know it," Sean said bitterly. "The government's just saving itself a little money by branding him a deserter."

"And sure, we don't want their wretched money, anyway," Mrs. Kelly said. "I take in laundry. The boys have their paper routes. Maggie and her sister, Peg, just found good jobs guttin' poultry at the market. The Kellys have always got by on their own hard work, and we always will. And tonight we're celebratin', so let's have no more sad talk. Da would want us to be happy on this day." As she said that, Mrs. Kelly turned away because tears had misted her eyes. She gave them a quick dab with her apron tails, then barked, "Bertie, Thomas, Edward, please take your places at the table!"

The "men," that is, all the males twelve and above, sat first. As man of the house, Sean was entitled to the chair at the head of the table, but he insisted that I sit there instead. The youngest children of both sexes were relegated to the far end of the long table where their chatter and rambunctious squirming wouldn't disturb the adults. Mrs. Kelly and the older girls plunked down heaping platters of food. Buttered cabbage, mashed turnips, and stovetop fried potato cakes were passed around. Mrs. Kelly carved the meat by the stovetop.

"I'm so glad you like mutton," Mrs. Kelly said, sawing on the meat with a long two-pronged fork and carving knife. "I asked Sean if he thought you'd prefer stuffed ox tongues, crubeens, or mutton."

"Crubeens?" Tommy blurted, puzzled.

"Pig's trotters," Mary said from halfway down the table, holding up her front hands like animal paws. "Ma makes them with carrots and onions."

"Ox tongue?" I asked. People ate that?

"Ah, melts in your mouth the way Ma makes it," Liam said excitedly. "She boils them for hours in leeks and garlic, then peels off the skin right at the table."

"Oh, mutton's fine," I said. Then I remembered the skull I had seen Mrs. Kelly take out of the broth. I couldn't really see what she was sawing on, but I could hear the knife repeatedly whack against a bone.

Molly set a plate in front of me with two fist-size slabs of pinkish meat drizzled with gravy. I wondered what part of the skull it came from. Plates quickly landed in front of Sean, Tommy, Hughie, Hammy, and Liam, as well. With the girls yet to be served, Mrs. Kelly quickly sat down and said a short grace.

At the word "Amen," Sean and his brothers snatched

up their knives and forks and began shovelling food into their mouths. Carefully, I took a tiny bite of cabbage. It was surprisingly good. In fact, it was excellent. Even in the days when we had a French cook in our kitchen, I had never tasted cabbage like this. The turnips and potato cakes were equally wonderful. I still couldn't bring myself to eat the slab of meat in front of me, especially with the thought of that grinning skull a few feet behind me.

"Don't you like mutton, dear?" Mrs. Kelly asked, noting that I hadn't touched the meat.

"Oh, no," I said, blushing. "I always save my favourite food for last." I made a big show of cutting the meat.

"Can I have some more?" a voice asked.

I looked over to see that Ed had already cleared his plate.

"Why, yes. I'm sure," Mrs. Kelly said. "And, Thomas, how about you?"

"Yes, please, ma'am," Tommy said.

"How much meat can there be on a single sheep's head?" I suddenly asked

"Sheep's head?" Mrs. Kelly repeated. "Oh, dear me! I've served you some mutton leg. I have a head on the boil for sheep jam. I could cut off the cheeks for you if you like, Bertie."

"Oh, no, the leg's perfect," I said, finally jamming the forkful of meat into my mouth. It tasted so good that I almost bit my own tongue.

"Ma's started selling sheep jam to one the market vendors," Liam said. "Over there they call it head cheese or brawn. We call it jam."

The mutton was so delicious that I was almost temped to try the sheep's cheeks. By the time Mrs. Kelly had served Ed his second piece, I, too, was looking for seconds. We finished the meal with tea and bread and butter pudding. After dinner we gathered around the fireplace. Most of the Kelly girls played musical instruments ranging from fiddles and harps to a flat instrument I mistook for a tambourine but which turned out to be a drum.

Mrs. Kelly hadn't lied. Sean had a lovely singing voice. He started with a jig called "Mairie's Wedding" that made Mary blush because she obviously had taken a fancy to Ed. The next song was "A Bunch of Wild Thyme," which had a chorus that all the Kellys joined in on with glee. Sean's next tune, "Four Green Fields," was a sad ditty about an old woman who had lost her four sons fighting the English. Even I had a hard time keeping back the tears by the time Sean had signed off on that one.

Before long it was ten o'clock and time to go home or else we'd miss the last streetcar back. We survived a last crushing hug from Mrs. Kelly and said our goodbyes to the rest of the family. As the door closed behind us, I saw Mrs. Kelly lighting a fresh candle in front of her husband's photograph. When the door was completely shut, the lights went out.

"Wow!" Ed cried. "I'm blind."

"Give your eyes a few seconds to adjust," Sean said. He and Hughie were walking us to the streetcar to make sure we didn't get lost. "Things look different in the dark."

*Or in time,* I thought. Even four hours ago I wouldn't have believed I'd have taken pleasure in a Kelly's company. Suddenly, I felt quite fond of all of them. In the darkness we heard a man and woman having a drunken argument and neighbours shouting at them to shut up. A dog barked and was answered by a dozen others. A bottle smashed against a brick wall and something yelped.

When our eyes adjusted to the gloom, we started walking. Eventually, we came to the alley where all the animal excrement lurked. Now, in complete darkness, it would be a miracle if we emerged from the other end with clean shoes. Somewhere a church clock chimed the quarter hour.

"We're going to miss our streetcar," I warned.

"You guys ever been to the circus?" Sean asked, his white teeth glowing in the moonlight.

"Yes," we all said.

"Good, then follow me," Sean said. "It's a shortcut." He jumped onto some wooden crates stacked like steps and scaled an eight-foot-tall wooden fence. Spreading his arms like a high-wire walker, he balanced his way along the top of a fence that separated two backyards. Hughie followed right behind him. Tommy and Ed were next, then me. The fence was about two inches wide at the top, so it wasn't hard to balance, especially after six weeks of hanging off the *Marinion*'s runner beam.

We easily navigated the first thirty feet. "Now comes the fun part," Sean said as he stepped over into the next set of yards. Something black, heavy, and making a whirring noise rushed forward in the darkness and slammed against the fence below our feet.

"That's Cannonball," Sean told us as the creature backed up and charged the wall again. "He's a Rottweiler. You can see where he gets his name."

"Here comes Gargantua," Hughie murmured calmly as another black shape bounded toward us from the other yard. "He's a German shepherd."

Unlike Cannonball, Gargantua didn't ram the wall. Instead he barked and tried to jump up to our level. Fortunately for us, the fence was a few inches too high for him to reach, but we did get a good look at flashing fangs as we passed.

"Here comes Louie," Sean told us as we crossed into the next yard.

"Louie?" Tommy said.

"He's a French poodle."

"Ah!" Ed said. "Here, Louie, Louie!" He was answered by loud barking as a massive, curly-haired white dog snapped at his feet. Because Ed had called its name, the dog took a particular interest in him, following all the way along the fence as it barked and tried to sink its teeth into Ed.

"Standard-bred poodle," I said. "The French use them for deer hunting."

"Thanks, Simcoe," Ed said. "Next time tell me that first."

Two yards to go. More angry mutts of unspecified breeds but big teeth and an ugly attitude were common denominators. At the last yard Sean and Hughie paused.

"Now this is my favourite," Sean said. "On the right is Gustav McCool. He's an Irish wolfhound crossed with a Great Dane."

Tommy and Ed glanced back at me.

"Two of the biggest dogs in the world," I said.

"On the left is Minnie. She's a three-hundred-pound

Berkshire hog. Normally, she's easy to get along with, but she just had piglets and she'll rip the legs off anyone who comes near them. If you're going to fall, take your chances with McCool. Step lively, lads, especially you, Simcoe. McCool usually goes for the straggler."

I didn't have time to reflect on the fact that Sean had just used my friend's nickname for me. Without a word Sean and Hughie sprinted along the top of the fence, followed by Ed and Tommy. I trailed as fast as I could, but with all the racket we'd made getting this far, both Minnie and McCool were now waiting for us. The night air was filled with shrill pig squeals and baritone dog woofs as we raced along the fence. On the left, angry red pig eyes and three-inch yellowish tusks gleamed in the moonlight. On the right, in the shadow of the fence, McCool barked and scratched. On his hind legs he could almost reach the top of the fence with his huge head — fortunately, he was either too old or too colossal to jump.

A maple tree stood a few feet from the end of the fence. Sean leaped off at a full run, caught a tree branch like a trapeze artist, and lowered himself to the ground. One by one we followed his example until we were all standing on Queen Street. Behind us, barking dogs, squealing pigs, and cursing animal owners filled the evening air like a chorus.

"Here comes your streetcar," Hughie said.

"You guys are crazy," Ed panted out to Sean and Hughie in admiration.

Ed, Tommy, and I looked at one another for a second.

"We need crazy," Tommy said thoughtfully.

We let the streetcar go by.

# 12

# The Pennant

## February 23, 1907

The sky was clear, but the howling wind sounded like a broken pipe organ outside my bedroom window when I woke up Saturday morning. *It'll be cold out on the lake today* was my first thought, but winning the Durnan Cup warmed my spirits. My mother had made oatmeal for breakfast, and for once it wasn't burnt or undercooked. I took that as a good omen. Mom refused to come to the race, but she gave me a big hug at the door.

"Promise me you'll be careful," she said.

"Cross my heart," I replied. Father was standing there in his winter coat and fur hat. There was something different about him that I couldn't spot right away. Then it hit me. "You're not ..."

"Crying," Father finished with a smile. "Yes. The tears stopped yesterday when I handed in my notice at the warehouse. I accepted Mr. Russell's offer to work at Canadian Carriage and Motor."

"Your books ..."

"Can wait. The position I've accepted is part of a team. We'll be working on new bicycle designs, but the hours will be much more controlled. There will be plenty of time for reading in the evening when I come home."

Hwei and his uncle were waiting for us in the doorway of their shop. Mr. Coon said something to Hwei in Cantonese. Hwei smiled. "Uncle says we're crazy to sail in this weather."

I grinned at Hwei, and we began walking. There were no trolleys running this early on Saturday, so we walked briskly along Adelaide Street until we reached York Street.

With the wind blowing so hard, I more than half expected the race to be called off, but there were seven boats lined up on the ice at the foot of York and hundreds of spectators braving the wintry blasts of the wind. The *IT* was there, of course; Fred would race in a tornado if he thought he could catch one. Then there was the *Temeraire* with Willie Fisher and a crew of eight. He had obviously rounded up every man he could to add weight in this wind. There was also *First Attempt*, captained by Rick Price, a Toronto millionaire banker who had imported a custom-built, Kingston-style racing boat just for this competition. Price had spared no expense to make his boat as lightweight as it was strong. His mast and boom were made of hollow steel, and instead of canvas, his sail was fashioned from red silk. It he could stay upright, he would likely be a serious threat in this race.

Hector McDonell was present with his new boat, the *King Edward*, and Tommy and Ed were waiting with the *Marinion*. Ed and Tommy had spent two days sharpening the skates on the runners and making sure all the shrouds and stays were in perfect condition.

"Ten minutes to race start!" the Commodore announced through his megaphone.

Tommy seemed a little worried. There was still no sign of Isobel or the Kellys yet.

"They have the farthest to come," I reminded them. "They'll be here."

Tommy nodded but said nothing. I watched as two gunners from the local militia artillery battery set up a miniature cannon called a "grasshopper" to fire the start signal. A Queen's Own Rifles bugler nearly froze his lips trying to signal the "Five minutes to race" call.

Still no sign of Isobel or Sean.

"Gentlemen, take your marks," the Commodore said.

We had drawn fourth from the left spot, which placed us dead centre in the field. From left to right our opponents were the *Temeraire* and the *King Edward*, then *First Attempt*, the *Jack Frost*, the *Yankee Doodle*, and finally Fred's *IT* on the far right.

Ed took the port runner beam while Hwei and I lined up on the starboard. Tommy stood sadly at the stern, ready to push off when the cannon fired.

"One minute!" barked the Commodore.

"We'll give 'em hell, Tommy," Ed said encouragingly.

Tommy smiled bravely, but I knew what he was thinking. With only four crew members we were going to be spending more time fighting to stay upright than racing.

From the lakeshore came a series of rapidly approaching honks. Many people gazed skyward, expecting a flight of geese to pass overhead. Instead, a large blue limousine surged over the brink of the shore and slid down the bank like a toboggan. Mr. DeSalle was driving; his wife and Isobel were beside him. Sean,

Hughie, the chauffeur, and a half-dozen Kellys were clinging to the running boards. As soon as the vehicle came to a halt, all the doors flew open and more Kellys poured out from every direction.

Sean and Hughie hit the ground running, but they were still beaten to their posts by Isobel. "We stopped to pick up Sean and Hughie," she said breathlessly. "When we offered to bring Sean's mother along, too, to watch, they insisted on bringing everyone."

Kellys were still climbing out of the car when the Commodore announced that the race would begin in fifteen seconds. A crumpled-looking Fräulein von Tirpitz was the last one out, trying to pry Liam off her leg with an umbrella.

Hughie and Sean joined Ed and me on the runners. Sean clapped a bowler hat on my head to replace the one I had lost in the ice hole. He smirked. "Don't ask where that came from."

Back among the spectators I could see a bald businessman holding his bare head and searching the ground.

"Three!" the Commodore bellowed.

Fine ice particles blowing off the island stung our cheeks as if the wind were cueing up for the race, as well.

"Two!"

"Good luck, *Marinion*!" Hector McDonell called out from the *King Edward*.

"Good luck, *King Edward*!" Tommy yelled back.

"One!"

"God's speed!" Mrs. Kelly's voice shrilled as the cannon fired.

The crowd roared in unison as seven crews kicked their feet furiously and the boats moved forward. Seven sails opened with a fusillade of snaps, and the boats took off like a flock of geese.

*First Attempt* scored the first error of the race as the powerful wind caught the boat's huge sail and the vessel took off but left two bank clerks running behind. Captain Price had to choose between slowing down to let them board or keep going. He decided on the latter. The two clerks trudged back to the starting point sheepishly.

The first buoy was at Mugg's Landing just off the northwestern tip of the islands. To reach it we had to sail southwest with a strong wind blowing solidly from York Street. Tommy swung the boom to starboard. Ed, Hwei, and Hammy climbed out on the port runner, while Hughie and I leaned left from the main beam.

"Washboard dead ahead!" Isobel cried from the ratlines. "Steer starboard twenty yards!"

Tommy steered slightly to starboard, and we gained one place as other boats shook violently as they passed over the rough ice.

The race was already heating up. The first three craft, the *King Edward*, *First Attempt*, and the *IT* were barely a dozen feet apart as they rounded the Mugg's Landing buoy at fifty miles per hour. The next leg of the race was to the Eastern Gap, which meant we were heading directly into the wind. The speeds diminished, but the race became a game of chicken as the boats started tacking back and forth and bows and runners just missed one another by inches.

I was farthest out on the port runner when I saw *Temeraire*'s starboard runner come straight at me. There was nowhere to go, so I hung on tight and watched in horrific fascination as we closed for impact. At the last second Tommy hiked us up to starboard six feet, and the *Temeraire*'s runner passed below us in a blur. There was no time to think about what had just happened.

"Stand by for a port tack!" Tommy shouted, and we all switched sides on the boat again.

Rounding the Eastern Gap buoy was another danger. Once boats turned northwest, they had the gale-force east wind fully behind them and took off like bullets. If any boat blundered into another's path as it accelerated, there would be an ugly crash. *Yankee Doodle* just missed us as it cut us off, and Tommy had to let out some wind until the *Doodle* was out of the way.

Fred Phelan had begun from the worst starting point, but he was already in second place as the *IT* moved quickly ahead of the pack. Phelan trailed only the *King Edward*, but he was giving Tommy's father a close race. Suddenly, the Kingston boat, *First Attempt*, shot past the *Marinion* as if we were standing still and bore down on the *IT* and the *King Edward*.

"Wow!" Ed yelled as we watched the three boats round the York buoy in a tightly packed formation.

"Sixty miles per hour!" Isobel announced from the mast, but it felt like nothing compared to watching the *IT* and *First Attempt* steal first and second place from the *King Edward*. The roar of the crowd from the shore woke us up as we realized we were about to make a port turn at a mile per minute or hit the ice piled up along the embankment.

Tommy twisted the tiller hard. We all braced for the tight turn. Hughie lost his footing, and Hwei and Ed caught him by an armpit each or he would have joined the two bank clerks from *First Attempt*, who were now cheering with the rest of the spectators on the shore.

It appeared to be a three-boat tie for first place as the *IT*, the *King Edward*, and *First Attempt* closed in on the Mugg's Landing buoy for the second time. We again steered starboard to avoid the washboard and were gaining on the leaders when suddenly we saw the *King Edward* veer leeward.

"He's lost his starboard skate!" Isobel called out as Tommy looked on in concern while his father fought to gain control of the bucking boat. The high wind showed no mercy, and the *King Edward* skidded right before finally coming to rest on its side a few yards from shore. Hector and his crew quickly stood and waved to show that all was well as we shot past the Mugg's Landing buoy and began the tacking leg again.

Willie Fisher in the *Temeraire* had managed to sneak past us while Tommy had watched what was happening to the *King Edward*, so now we concentrated on closing the gap with him. Fisher was normally a cautious skipper, but the constant howling wind and the abnormally high speed seemed to take possession of him. He and his crew started executing a series of high-speed tacks, each one more spectacular and dangerous than the last.

With each new hard tack, Fisher glanced back at us, his eyes flashing in triumph as the *Temeraire* began hiking on alternating runners like a speed skater, his crew bravely straining to keep the boat upright. But

Fisher took one chance too many. In the process of changing tack, a fluke gust of wind caught the *Temeraire* in mid-turn and flipped it like a toy. Crewmen flew in all directions. We roared past the wreckage, followed by the *Yankee Doodle* and the *Jack Frost*.

The *Marinion* was now in third place behind the *IT* and *First Attempt*. We were running so close that the crewmen on the runners could have swapped boats just by stepping sideways a few inches.

"Best race ever!" Phelan cried out.

We weren't sure if he was talking to us, his crew, or the *IT*. Again *First Attempt* began to pull ahead of us as its extra-large sail took advantage of the wind, but the rough ice on this leg was taking a toll on the Kingston boat. The port skate bent dangerously to the inside, and the lightweight steering gear was straining under Price's weight. Suddenly, the tiller broke, making the boat yaw left and right at high speed. Phelan and Tommy immediately spilled wind out of sails as *First Attempt* zigzagged perilously in front of both vessels. Price finally veered far enough to port so that we could dodge past *First Attempt*, and both the *IT* and the *Marinion* resumed full speed. Incredibly, as we rounded the York Street buoy for the second time, we saw the *Temeraire* back in the race. Fisher and his crew had righted their boat and clawed back into the race. They were trailing the pack by almost a lap, but with this wind anything could happen.

Because of the way *First Attempt* crossed the *IT*'s bow, Tommy was able to grab full wind, and we seized the lead before Phelan could do the same. We were now in first place with one lap to go. But the wind was still gaining strength, and the *Marinion* was struggling just to hold together. Where the mast bench met the centre timber the thumb-size bolts were squeaking shrilly as they strained to hold the mast in place. Isobel still looked as cool as a high tea cucumber sandwich even while the mast she clung to moaned and creaked in the wind.

"Attaboy, Tommy, go! Go! Go!" Hector and his crew hollered as we rounded the Mugg's Landing buoy, still leading the *IT* by six lengths. Even over the wind we could hear the crowd on the shore cheer.

"Seventy miles an hour!" Isobel cried from the topmast. She had that darn watch out again.

"We don't even have the wind full on our beam yet," Tommy told us. "We might hit eighty or ninety before this race is over."

And ninety miles an hour still might not win the race. The *IT* was hot on our stern, and Phelan's crew were singing their victory chant as we rounded the Eastern Gap buoy locked runner to runner.

"Straight for home, boys!" Phelan bellowed.

"Let's feed them our spray!" Tommy yelled.

With the wind on our starboard beams both boats picked up speed. Phelan was running on our leeward side, nearest the shore. Both crews had every available hand on the starboard side of their respective boats. Hwei, Hughie, and Ed were on our starboard runner beam. Sean and I were fighting to keep our bums from hitting the ice as we leaned back to prevent the *Marinion* from capsizing. Then a fluke side wind bounced off the shore and caught the *IT* abeam.

We heard a cry from the crew on the *IT* as it hiked up on the port and stern blades. Even with two full-grown men on the starboard runner, its blade was six feet off the ground and still rising.

"She's gonna flip!" Ed screamed over the howling wind.

The *IT*'s beam rose another four feet until the boat was sailing nearly sideways and the crewmen were standing on the side of the vessel. The two hands on the starboard beam were actually hanging off to the right side of the blade. Standing sideways in his cockpit, Phelan somehow stopped the *IT* from capsizing. Like a wagon balanced on two wheels, the *IT* streaked across the ice, still heading for the finish line at full speed.

Craning our necks, we watched in fascination as one fearless *IT* crewman let go of his safety lines, turned, and shimmied up the nearly vertical starboard beam as if it were a coconut tree. His added weight slowly moving to starboard lowered the runner toward the ice, but another fluke gust could flip the *IT* at any time.

The roar of the crowd brought our attention back to our own situation. The finish line was three hundred yards away. We were running bow-to-bow with the *IT*, so with all our collective strength we hauled the sail closer for maximum speed.

"Haul her just a little bit closer," Tommy said, and Sean and I pulled back on the sheet a few more inches.

The *Marinion* surged forward a little faster, but suddenly a sickening tearing sound erupted over our heads. *Bwwaaaarrrrre!* I glanced up and saw our sail rip in half from leech to luft. The canvas couldn't stand the strain.

Released from the high wind pressure, the boom snapped back to starboard like a catapult arm. It would have definitely taken my head clean off if Sean hadn't smacked me down with a backhand. The boom still managed to clip the brim of my bowler hat, sending it flying across the ice. I didn't have time to thank Sean because a noise from above made us gaze topside.

*"Whooooooooeeeeee!"* Isobel squealed as she dodged the flapping spar like a trapeze artist.

"She's crazy," Sean said.

"We're all crazy," I said.

With our sail flapping in the wind we cruised to a halt and watched helplessly as the *IT* finally put its runner onto the ice and easily shot across the finish line for first place.

The *Yankee Doodle* and the *Jack Frost* were out of the race, so it was between us and the *Temeraire* for second and third. The *Temeraire* was just rounding the Eastern Gap buoy. We were only a hundred yards from the finish line, but we were dead on the ice and weren't allowed to push the *Mārinion*.

"Great race, guys," Tommy said sadly. "Shame we can't finish it."

"We gave her a good run," Ed said, but I could tell he was crushed, too.

Suddenly, Hwei jumped off the runner and ran back to the mast. "We can make a junk sail."

"The sail's already junk," Tommy said.

Hwei pointed at the boom and spar. "No, a junk sail!"

"He means a junk-style sail like they use in China," I said. "They use battens between short pieces of canvas.

Tommy and Ed stared at me quizzically.

Isobel slid down from the ratlines. "I know what Hwei means. Let's try it."

We had to work fast. Following Hwei's instructions, Tommy dropped the luff boom to half mast. Hwei pulled out his knife and started making holes along a folded seam at the bottom of what was left of the *Marinion*'s upper sail. Isobel and I wove a rope from the foot boom through the holes Hwei was creating so that we had a short, wide sail shaped like a quadrangle.

"Here comes the *Temeraire*!" Ed yelled.

We all looked. Fisher's battered iceboat was picking up speed at the Eastern buoy.

"Hurry!" Tommy cried.

"Almost finished," Hwei said.

We could hear the crowd chanting the names of our two boats.

"Finished," I said, tying off the boom rope as well as I could.

"Okay, all aboard!" Tommy ordered.

We swung the sail into the wind. For a few seconds nothing happened.

"The blades are frozen to the ice," Ed said.

"We're allowed to push off again," Tommy said, and we assumed our push-off positions.

"Heave!" Ed shouted.

We strained, but the boat refused to move. The *Marinion* seemed nailed to the ice.

"Again!" Ed urged. "Heave!" Small, ripping noises were heard from below as the blades broke free. "Push!"

Tommy trimmed the sail to catch the maximum

wind. The *Marinion* began to move forward again under its own power.

"All aboard!" we all joyfully cried.

The *Temeraire* was closing fast, but we were picking up speed. Not much speed, but we were travelling and the finish line was now only fifty yards ahead.

"Go! Go! Go! Go!" the spectators chanted at the finish line. People were calling out the names of the boats and individual members of the sailing crew. We were now at maximum speed, progressing at the pace of a trotting horse and wagon. I glanced back and saw the *Temeraire* over my shoulder about to streak past us. The finish line was ten feet ahead....

"That several people were not killed or maimed in yesterday's iceboat race ... is a mystery to those who were in or saw the race. Of seven boats which started, only three were able to finish the course," Mr. DeSalle read to us the next day as we sat in his parlour sipping tea. He was reading a *Toronto Daily Star* reporter's account of the race and continued.

> "The wind picked up to gale force. It blew so hard that every boat in the fleet reefed down except Phelan's *IT* and William Fisher's *Temeraire.* Phelan wouldn't reef if it blew a cyclone and Fisher couldn't because his sail has no reef points. Better judgment told Fisher to remain a spectator, but someone taunted him with

yellowness, and he promptly brought his boat to the mark just to show his detractor that there wasn't a jaundiced spot on his whole epidermis. 'We'll sail the course or come back in matchwood,' said Fisher.

"*King Edward*, while going out to the first buoy at a speed of over a mile a minute, broke her leeward skate off the runner plank and went careening down to leeward, tearing and leaping to and fro like a locoed bronco.

"*Temeraire*, going over at the Mugg's Landing buoy when she was in the grip of a fierce squall, turned a flip and sent her crew of eight flying in all directions. Just imagine a boat going at sixty-five miles an hour turning over and stop to figure out how far the men who were clinging to her are going to go before they land. *Temeraire* went over and scattered her crew over an acre of solid ice, yet every man jack of them was able to scramble to his feet.

"*First Attempt* was giving *Marinion* and *IT* a run for their money when her steering apparatus gave out. She yawed crazily about and, after making a merry-go-round of herself, consented to stand still and let the other races go by.

"It was Phelan, however, who almost ended up as kindling.

"*IT* went away with a jump that boded ill for her rivals. A fierce puff caught her from out of John Street, and she reared up on two skates. There were two men out on the blade, but they could not begin to hold her down. Up she went, and up some more until the skate was ten feet off the ice. Her sheet was hastily slackened but she overed up on two blades until it seemed that nothing would save her. It was not until a couple more men pulled their weight out to weather on her, and her sail was flapping, that she came back to the ice. She landed with a bump, picked up her speed, and crossed the finish line.

"*Marinion* was doing well, but her rotten canvas commenced to tear at the reef points and young Tom and his 'kid' crew appeared to be finished until some ingenious repairs allowed them to limp across the finish line just a hair's breadth behind the *Temeraire* who amazingly returned to the race. So Phelan's *IT* takes the pennant this year, *Temeraire* returns from the dead to place second, and *Marinion* refuses to say die and takes a very close third.

"Strenuous sport, this Hard Water Sailing."

"Third place," Mr. DeSalle said, lowering the newspaper. "A very impressive achievement, especially under the circumstances."

Sean sighed. "We came so close to winning."

"That's the thrill and the heartbreak of sailboat racing," Mr. DeSalle said. "On any day any boat can be a winner or a loser depending on skill and luck."

"If only I could have afforded a new sail instead of hoping that old rag would get us through," Tommy said.

"*First Attempt* was brand-new from bow to stern," Isobel said. "They didn't even finish the race."

"There's always next year," I said.

"There's always next year!" Tommy and Ed echoed, raising their teacups for a toast.

"With the third-place prize money we can build a better boat," Tommy said. "More important, we've already got the crew. We'll win for sure next year."

"Everybody still crazy enough to race next year?" Ed asked.

Hughie, Sean, Hwei, and I immediately answered yes, but there was an awkward silence from Isobel. I noticed that she gave her parents a sad glance.

"Isobel?" Tommy asked.

For once it was Isobel blushing. "I'm afraid we're going away again."

"Away? Where?" Sean demanded.

"Buenos Aires," Mr. DeSalle said. "And then back to New York perhaps. And after that who knows?"

"Buenos Where-as?" Ed asked.

"Argentina," Hughie said.

Everyone gaped at him.

He shrugged. "I have no idea how I knew that."

His last remark broke the tension in the room as everyone laughed.

"Must be from hanging around Lord Simcoe so much," Ed quipped.

"But why are you leaving us, Isobel?" Sean asked. I think, like the rest of us, he was smitten with her.

"My fault, I'm afraid," Mr. DeSalle said. "My company's sending me to investigate the profitability of beef futures in South America. We'll be leaving in three weeks."

"Three weeks!" the male members of the *Marinion*'s crew moaned in unison.

"I ... I don't know what to say," Isobel said miserably. "In my life I've moved more than two dozen times, but I've never felt the pang of leaving so much as today."

"You've got to go where your family goes," Sean said. "Family's everything."

"I know, but you all seem like family now, too," Isobel said.

"We may return some day," Fräulein von Tirpitz added. She looked pretty unhappy, too, at the thought of leaving Ed.

"We'll meet again," Mr. DeSalle said. "Things have a way of coming full circle."

13

# The Market

## December 24, 1907

"Run, Bertie!" Mr. Crane cried. He had just spotted Sean Kelly approaching from the north door.

I hesitated. I had a porcupine in each hand.

"Gimme those!" Hughie Kelly ordered, holding out his hands.

I glanced at Mr. Crane. He nodded, and I carefully handed over the porcupines. "Mind the tails," I said as I stripped off my apron.

Carefully, Hughie took the porcupines and started wrapping them for the customer I had been serving. Hughie and I both had part-time jobs at Mr. Crane's for the holidays.

"You coming, McCross?" Sean asked, passing by the stall without pausing.

I nodded goodbye to Mr. Crane and Hughie, then slid under the counter. "You're early."

Sean nodded. "Yeah, a bit. Have to stop off and see Ma before we go."

We dodged and weaved through the Christmas crowds.

"Hi, Sean! Hi, Bertie," Kelly voices called from

behind nearly every counter. Liam saluted us from a cheese counter. Patrick and Mike waved bunches of carrots at us like flags from a produce aisle on the other side.

Although we hadn't won the Durnan Cup the previous winter, "Tommy McDonell and His Kid Crew" had become celebrities for just finishing the race. Since then, with Tommy's recommendations, nearly every Kelly kid old enough to dodge a truant officer had found steady employment in the St. Lawrence Market. With the money pouring in, Mrs. Kelly herself had been able to open a stall that sold Irish delicacies. Her eldest daughters, Shauna, Megan, Meg, and Tara, worked with her.

"Hi, Ma," Sean greeted. "How's the sheep jam selling?" He put his pay packet on the counter. Sean had become an apprentice cook at one of the nearby hotels.

Mrs. Kelly slipped the envelope into her apron pocket. "Fine. Where's Bertie?" she demanded, looking worried.

"Hi, Ma," I said. "Merry Christmas!" I handed her a penny rose I had purchased for half price because it was closing time on Christmas Eve.

"Ah, me darlin'," Mrs. Kelly said.

She always insisted on my calling her "Ma" the way her own boys did. At the sight of that silly little flower, her huge face quivered, then crumpled in an avalanche of happy tears. I was thankful for three feet of chest-high steel counter between us or else I'd be getting another spine-busting bear hug.

*"Ahhhhhh!"* the Kelly girls chorused.

What was it with women and flowers? I had no idea, but I had a feeling the knowledge would serve me well in the future — better than anything I'd ever learn out of a book.

"Hey, Simcoe! Sweet Potato!" Ed called from the south entrance. "The ice ain't getting any warmer."

"Gotta go, Ma," Sean said.

"Don't forget," Mrs. Kelly reminded us. "Sean's singin' his solo at midnight Mass tonight."

"We'll be there," I promised as Molly handed over a wicker basket full of soup jars well padded with rags to keep them warm and unbroken. I couldn't help but sneak a peek. Ox tongue, my favourite! Jars clinking, we crossed the railway tracks and slid down the dirt embankment to the market canal.

Hwei was already out on the ice talking to Tommy. Beside them was the new iceboat we had built partly from salvaged bits of the *Marinion* and partly from new lightweight masts and spars I was able to scrounge through my father at the CCM plant. Thomas Russell had taken a keen interest in iceboat racing and had given us the parts free if we promised to send back notes on how well they performed.

Tommy and Ed had already taken the boat on a few test spins around the ice to adjust the rigging correctly, but this was the first time the whole crew was about to set sail on a real run.

"Did you bring it?" Tommy asked.

I nodded and fished in my pocket to produce a small bottle of real French champagne.

"When he heard about our new boat, he sent it

special delivery," I said, handing the bottle to Tommy.

"Thank you, Mr. DeSalle," Tommy said, holding the bottle up to the moon. "Let's get cracking."

We stood in a line facing the boat.

"I hereby christen this new iceboat the *Isobel*," Tommy intoned. "May she always find a fair wind and smooth ice." With a loud whack Tommy hit the bow with the bottle, but it bounced off. He gave it another whack. Again it bounced off.

Ed laughed. "Gee, she's being difficult already."

"With a name like *Isobel* what did you expect?" Tommy asked in exasperation. "Here, Simcoe, you try it." He handed the bottle to me.

My father had told me there was a certain technique for cracking a champagne bottle. "They're made to withstand tremendous pressure at either end," he had said. "Try hitting it on the shoulder where the glass is thinnest."

That was exactly what I did, and the bottle exploded in one motion. Champagne splashed over the boat's bow, and the tinkle of glass landing on the ice reminded me of Isobel's laugh. As if on cue, a moderate wind blew up from the southeast.

"Let's sail," Tommy said, and we pushed the boat backward down the bank onto the ice, turned her about, and assumed the launch position.

"Go!" Tommy cried.

Although this wasn't a race, we pushed forward as if Fred Phelan and the *IT* were waiting for us at Mugg's Landing. Tommy hauled up the sail, and we scrambled aboard as the *Isobel*'s silk sail caught the wind gracefully and a slow but steady acceleration under our feet resulted.

"She moves like a dream," Sean said.

Because this was a pleasure cruise, I sat in the wicker cockpit next to Tommy and Ed.

"Have you heard from her lately?" Tommy asked me as we skirted the north shoreline. He didn't have to say who.

"Yeah, she sent me a letter last week," I said. "Apparently, they're back in New York now. She and her parents were invited to sail the Hudson River with President Teddy Roosevelt on the *Icicle*, his cousin's ice yacht."

"An ice yacht?" Ed asked.

"Yeah," I said. "It's quite the rig. Twin masts, sixty-nine feet long, with more than a thousand square feet of canvas. They were losing a race against some other millionaire named Rogers until Isobel climbed the front mast and began calling out ice conditions to the crew below."

"What did the president say?" Tommy asked.

"Bully! Whatever that's supposed to mean. Because of her, they won the race, she says."

Tommy nodded. "Of course. Never any doubts in that girl's mind."

"After New York they're off to Tokyo and Moscow for a year," I said.

"Tokyo?"

"Yeah, Japan just handed Russia its keister in a naval war, and Mr. DeSalle's company thinks there's money to be made investing in both countries."

Tommy sighed. "Is she ever coming back?"

"I hope so," I said.

Tommy changed tack, and as we luffed, the silk sail rustled like a woman's dress. We hit a small pressure crack. Instinctively, Tommy and I glanced up at the mast top. No Isobel, just the full moon shining down so brightly that I felt sure I could reach up and touch it.

# Other Books by Steve Pitt

**To Stand and Fight Together**
***Richard Pierpoint and the Coloured Corps of Upper Canada***
978-1-55002-731-0
$19.99

In 1812 a sixty-eight-year-old black United Empire Loyalist named Richard Pierpoint helped raise the Coloured Corps of Upper Canada. This unique combat corps saw service throughout the War of 1812 and was the first colonial military unit reactivated to quash the Rebellion of 1837. Pierpoint and the Coloured Corps are the central focus of the book, but sidebars featuring fascinating facts about the rise and fall of slavery in North America and the state of African Canadians in early Canada provide an entertaining and informative supplement.

**Day of the Flying Fox**
***The True Story of World War II Pilot Charley Fox***
978-1-55002-808-9
$19.99

In July 1944 in France, Canadian Second World War pilot Charley Fox spotted a black staff car, the kind usually employed to drive high-ranking Third Reich dignitaries. Already noted for his skill in dive-bombing and strafing the enemy, Fox went in to attack the automobile. As it turned out, the car contained Germany's General Erwin Rommel, the Desert Fox, and Charley likely succeeded in wounding him. Author Steve Pitt focuses on this seminal event in Charley Fox's life and in the war, but he also provides fascinating aspects of the period, including profiles of noted ace pilot Buzz Beurling and Great Escape architect Walter Floody, as well as sidebars about Hurricanes, Spitfires, and Messerschmitts.